Heart to Heart

by

Jan Scarbrough

Return to Legend

The Winchesters of Legend, TN

To Marylee –
I hear you have
a big heart.
Hope you enjoy!
Jan Scarbrough

Jan Scarbrough

Copyright © 2015 Jan Scarbrough
Scarbrough, Jan
Heart to Heart
Media > Books > Fiction > Romance Novels
Category/Tags: romance, contemporary, Legend
Tennessee, small town, animal communicator, pet psychic,
Smoky Mountains

Print ISBN: 978-0-9971919-0-5
1st Digital release: June 2014
Saddle Horse Press Digital release: December 2015
Saddle Horse Press Print release: February 2016

Editor, Gilly Wright
Cover Design by **www.Calliope-Designs.com**

This edition is published by agreement with Saddle Horse Press, PO Box 221543, Louisville, KY 40252.

DEDICATION

For my daughter Brenna—
a veterinarian who talks to animals in her own way.

Jan Scarbrough

Invitation for a free ebook

You have recently purchased a paperback copy of Heart to Heart. Maybe you bought it as a birthday or Christmas gift and might like to read it yourself.

If you send me via email a copy of your receipt, I will send you one of the following free ebook versions:

iBook

Kindle

PDF

How do you do this?

Simply scan the receipt from your print purchase or even easier, make a screenshot from your Amazon or B&N receipt. Via email, send the copy of your receipt to me at jan@janscarbrough.com.

Jan Scarbrough

HEART TO HEART

When Jeremy's aunt gives him a second chance, he must decide if he believes in the unbelievable and the pet psychic who teaches him about faith…and love.

Jeremy Hamilton's company is cash-strapped and his personal life is a mess. Inheriting the bulk of Ms. Addie Bynum's wealth is a godsend, but to get the money, Jeremy must move to the small town of Legend, Tennessee, a place that will remind readers of Cedar Cove and/or Virgin River. Ms. Addie has given Jeremy a second chance under certain conditions. Will he take that chance?

Marty Fields is a pet psychic. She's spent a lifetime explaining animal communication to skeptic citizens of her small town. Only Ms. Addie understands her gift. Keeping Ms. Addie's six cats after the old lady's death is the least Marty can do. Yet, she's put her life on hold. Will the grandnephew's arrival upset the rhythm of her comfortable existence?

Note: Legend, Tennessee, exists in the hearts of its readers, and the mind of its four authors—Magdalena Scott, Maddie James, Janet Eaves, and I. To date, we have thirty-plus stories that take place in this small town nestled in the Great Smoky Mountains. I hope you enjoy reading them.

Jan Scarbrough

The Legend Post-Dispatch Obituary

Mrs. Adeline Hamilton Bynum, 83, known to the Legend community as Ms. Addie, passed away on April 8 in the comfort of her home after a yearlong illness. A lifelong resident of Legend, she was preceded in death by an infant daughter Caroline, and her husband Roger Bynum, the owner of the Post-Dispatch and other community businesses.

Ms. Addie was a member of the Legend United Methodist Church where a public celebration of her life will be held on Sunday at 2:00 p.m. In life, Ms. Addie was a private woman, who enjoyed her rose garden and grew championship roses. Over the years, she also touched the lives of many children, participating in the county foster family program and giving part-time work to deserving teens. She also had a soft heart for stray animals. Cats were her favorite, but she also contributed to the local animal rescue charities.

A great-nephew, Jeremy Hamilton of Louisville, Kentucky, survives Ms. Addie. Memorial gifts can be made to the Legend Animal Shelter or Alley Cat Advocates (www.alleycatadvocates.org).

Jan Scarbrough

Chapter One

The law office of Graham Winchester
Downtown, Legend, Tennessee

"I don't understand." Jeremy Hamilton scooted forward in the leather guest chair. He frowned at the well-dressed lawyer seated behind a mahogany executive desk. "Are you saying I don't get the money right away?"

"I'm saying the money is tied up in a trust," Graham Winchester replied. He too sat forward in his high-back swivel chair. "Ms. Addie placed certain conditions on the money and her other assets."

Great.

Jeremy knew the man facing him was a famous novelist with two bestselling books, who had left his New York City law career for a wife and family in Legend. Not the smartest move, in Jeremy's mind, but then again, to each his own.

Live and let live had been Jeremy's motto for years. That was until his dad passed and he inherited the business, an agency for information technology contractors. Today Hamilton Staffing was in trouble. Big time. And no matter what Jeremy did, the economy conspired against him. The recent letter from this lawyer was a godsend. His great-aunt's money would pump needed cash into his cash-strapped company.

Winchester sat back and rested his elbows on the arms

of his executive chair, steepling his fingers thoughtfully at his tight lips. He swiveled back and forth slowly, his gaze resting on Jeremy as if sizing him up.

Too bad he wasn't back home in Louisville, Kentucky, or on a sandy Hawaiian beach, anywhere but this stuffy, uncomfortable office. Winchester's stare annoyed him. Jeremy's body temperature rose in response.

"But I need that money now," he said a little too sharply. "I need it to make my payroll."

It was hard to admit he was in one helluva fix. He only had two months' worth of capital left. Several large companies had failed to pay him, and so he couldn't provide the salaries promised to his contractors. Without an immediate influx of cash, he'd go under.

"I understand you were not close to Ms. Addie."

Winchester's statement had little to do with the issue at hand. Jeremy stiffened. "I barely knew her. My parents moved from Legend when I was a baby. We would visit occasionally, but after my grandparents died when I was fourteen, we never came again."

And then his father lost his job, and apparently, his mom couldn't handle the change. She deserted them once the money dried up, leaving Jeremy to be raised by his dad. He frowned at the memory. At the hurt and anger, the unfairness of it all. At the disloyalty of women. All women.

The irony of it all was his dad had started his own company and became more successful and wealthy than before the divorce.

Jeremy was proud of his dad and what he'd

accomplished. Now it was up to him to continue that success. To keep Hamilton Staffing going. People depended upon him. Technical people who'd lost their jobs because of the rotten economy had found work and hope through his company. He couldn't let them down, any more than he could let the memory of his father down.

"You are Ms. Addie's only living relative," Winchester stated. "Although she's left the bulk of her estate to you, she's bequeathed certain items to others and given money to her favorite animal rescue charities."

"Is that why I don't get the inheritance right away?"

"No." Winchester shook his head. "That part of the trust has nothing to do with what you will inherit."

Jeremy let out a frustrated sigh. "Then tell me. Don't beat around the bush."

Winchester sat forward and placed his hands on the desktop. "You receive the bulk of the estate when, and only when, her six cats pass."

"What?"

"Ms. Addie had six cats. They will live in her house at the expense of the trust until each one passes because of natural causes, or if their guardian decides for health reasons, as Ms. Addie put it, they should be sent across Rainbow Bridge."

"What?" Jeremy couldn't believe what he was hearing. "That's crazy."

"You didn't know Ms. Addie. She was a bit eccentric."

Jeremy rolled his eyes. "You think? What's this

5

Rainbow Bridge thing?"

"The way I understand it is that pet lovers like to quote a poem called 'Rainbow Bridge' as being the place where their pets go after they die to wait for their owners."

"That *is* nuts."

Winchester shrugged. "Not to people like Ms. Addie."

The cat thing was too much. Too stupid for words. "I suppose I can't send them across this bridge myself."

The lawyer grinned. "You're right. Ms. Addie was concerned enough about that to appoint a guardian to look after the cats' best interests. The guardian, a Miss Martha Fields, who happens to be my second cousin, lives with the cats."

"You're kidding? Someone lives with the cats?"

"Ms. Addie gave Marty permission to live on the third story of the house so she'd be closer to them."

Jeremy's neck was stiff, and his head pounded. He'd driven five hours to Legend this morning just to have his hopes dashed by this crazy old woman's cats?

Unbelievable.

Winchester pushed his chair back from the desk and cocked his head. "When Ms. Addie's health took a turn for the worse six months ago, she asked me to find out about you."

Jeremy glared at the lawyer. "You were snooping on me?"

"Let's just say, I did a little research. Nothing the

Internet couldn't facilitate."

"So?" This was going from bad to worse.

"I learned you're single, recently out of a long-term relationship."

Jeremy's body tensed.

"I also learned about your financial difficulties," Winchester continued. "I found out that you work most of the time."

"So? There's a law against hard work?"

Winchester ignored the sarcasm. "After I told Ms. Addie, she expressed her desire that you, as she put it, 'stop and smell the roses.'"

"What does that mean?" Jeremy asked, squinting in anger.

"Ms. Addie added another clause to her trust, stating if you move into her house in Legend for a month and live there so her cats will come to accept you, then the money, except what is actually needed to take care of the cats, can be released to you."

Jeremy stood up and paced back and forth in front of the desk. His blood boiled. This was the most preposterous thing he'd ever heard. "Let me get this straight. I have to live in her house for a month?"

"Yes."

"And Ms. Addie was in her right mind?"

"Sharp as a tack."

"How do you know the cats will accept me?" Jeremy

quizzed. "Can you read their minds?"

"No," Winchester said. His voice was as bland as his expression. "But Marty does."

"Huh?" Jeremy stopped and faced the lawyer.

"Marty Fields talks to them."

Heart pounding, Jeremy stared in disbelief. "What?" His one word question ended on a piercing high note.

"Marty Fields talks to the cats," Winchester repeated. "Like Dr. Doolittle. She's an animal communicator."

Chapter Two

Winchester's law office was on the second floor of the bank and trust building on North Main. Jeremy exited the building by the rear door and slid into the driver's side of his black Acura RLX. He sat for a moment mulling over the conditions of the will.

He'd made his mind up rather quickly to accept the terms of Ms. Addie's late addition to her trust. After all, what choice did he have? He needed the damn money. The lawyer made it perfectly clear this was the only way he'd get his inheritance any time soon. One of the damn cats had just turned two years old. Didn't some cats live to be twenty?

No telling how long that young sucker could live.

And what was he supposed to do about his allergy to cats?

Absolutely f'ing amazing.

He turned the key in the ignition, shifted the vehicle into gear, and drove through the parking lot, passing the Piggly Wiggly on the corner, and turning right on Second Street. He'd seen some of Main Street on his way to the meeting. Little remained of what he remembered. Legend, Tennessee, had gotten a face-lift recently. It was no longer the sleepy little town of his childhood, but a quaint, Gatlinburg-like place peppered with bourbon barrels filled with petunias and geraniums and sidewalks lined with trees.

Some people might say the town was charming.

He wouldn't go that far. To him, Legend, Tennessee, was a means to an end. He had an operation to run, and although he could do it online via the Internet and his iPhone, Jeremy would rather be at his office, hands-on, managing the daily ups and downs of what was a successful business. That is, if he didn't run out of money as his accountant had warned.

Ms. Addie's house was somewhere near the community golf course. In fact, her husband had donated the land to the town to build the links. Jeremy didn't play golf. As far as he was concerned, it was a waste of time and energy. His father had played and had even made some of his best deals over a game of golf.

Fine.

To each his own. Jeremy had a more direct approach to business and little patience for the sport.

Glancing at his GPS, he turned onto Amber Street. When it morphed into Kyle Street, he watched for a gated entrance. Halfway down the block, there it was. The iron gates were swung wide open, as if he was expected. Jeremy turned into the entrance and followed the gently curving driveway to the summit. When he came around the last corner, Ms. Addie's rambling, Victorian home leaped out at him.

Wow!

The white house was massive, three stories tall, with a wide porch that wrapped around three sides. Green trim gave the exterior a striking, fresh look. The driveway took him to the side of the house. He pulled to a stop in front of a three-car garage, all his. The place was big and welcoming and all his.

Eventually.

He slung open the door, got out, and stood for a moment taking in the scenery. The front lawn of the house sloped downward giving him a view of the golf greens farther downhill. Mature trees flanked the side of the house opposite the driveway. As he followed the sidewalk to the porch steps, Jeremy noticed a sleek black cat sunning itself. When the cat spotted him, it slipped silently away into the bushes.

Good. Stay away from me.

This month was going to be rough. Something to be endured. Like a chemistry test in school or a root canal. Jeremy clenched his jaw at the thought. He wished he was somewhere else, but that wasn't going to happen. He had accepted his fate.

Just because he was allergic to cats and basically hated all animals, especially cats—the sly, sneaking creatures—didn't mean he couldn't survive the test Ms. Addie had left for him. He was strong-willed, if nothing else. Six cats would *not* best him.

He walked around the porch to the front door. Inhaling deeply and then exhaling through his mouth, Jeremy pressed the doorbell and waited.

***

Sunlight streamed through the frosted windows of the French doors and glistened on the hardwood floor of the entrance foyer. Marty Fields stood a moment in front of the door collecting herself. The shadow behind the windowpanes had to be Ms. Addie's great-nephew whose arrival Graham had alerted her to a few minutes earlier.

A longhaired, pale gray and white cat swiped Marty's bare legs with her tail and stepped gingerly over her bare feet. "Yes, Tinkerbelle," she thought. "That must be Ms. Addie's relative."

The young cat purred in response as it rubbed back-and-forth against her. Sucking in a breath for courage, Marty grasped the two doorknobs and turned them, throwing open both the French doors.

The glare of the sun threw the figure of a tall man into shadow. He cleared his throat, staring at her. "I'm Jeremy Hamilton," he said in a deep voice.

"I know." Marty dropped her gaze to the cat circling her legs. She stepped back to allow the nephew into the house, and as he entered the foyer, she lifted her gaze.

He was a good-looking man with close-cropped, brown hair and sparkling blue eyes—like a young Harrison Ford. He wore a trimmed beard, like many other young men. His silk power tie was red, and his dark gray suit expensive-looking.

"Meow," the cat greeted, transferring her attention to the guest and giving him the same leg rubbing treatment.

Jeremy looked down with something akin to horror on his face. He sidestepped but couldn't shake the persistent cat.

Marty grinned slightly, amused by his reaction.

"Tinkerbelle thinks you don't like her," she said softly.

Jeremy's mouth dropped open, and then he shut it. With a quick frown, he said, "I'm not used to cats."

"That's okay. Tink just wants to be your friend."

His breath hitched. His bushy eyebrows lifted. "You must be Ms. Fields."

"Marty." She stuck out her hand. "Nice to meet you."

Although hesitant at first, his handshake was firm. Marty liked the feel of his grasp. His hands were accustomed to giving direction and commanding results. But the initial uncertainty in his grip verified what Graham had already told her—the great-nephew was here only because Ms. Addie had made it impossible for him to be anywhere else.

Jeremy dropped his hand. "Did Mr. Winchester tell you why I'm here?"

She nodded. "I know all about your visit."

He squared his shoulders. "Then you know I'm supposed to live here for a month and get to know...ah...the cats."

"I know that too."

He studied her, his gaze moving from her face down her body and up again. "It's important to me, to my business, that I receive my inheritance as soon as possible."

Lifting her eyebrows at his forthrightness, Marty cocked her head. "I lived with your aunt the last year of her life. I understood her wishes in the matter."

His hands briefly clenched, and he scowled at her. "What I need you to understand is you have the ability to decide my fate and that of my employees and contractors. People who depend upon me. I don't like that."

She shrugged. Marty sensed his serious side, but when he gave her a thin-lipped smile, his eyes narrowing, she also sensed his intensity and determination. This guy was desperate. He'd been honest with her and deserved the same himself.

"You're wrong, Mr. Hamilton."

"Jeremy," he interrupted.

"Well, Jeremy." She shrugged again. "Your inheritance is in *your* hands, not mine. I can simply tell Graham what I hear from Ms. Addie's cats. If they don't like you, I can't lie about it."

He looked crestfallen for an instant, and then his expression turned earnest. "Help me out here, Marty," he begged. "I don't know anything about animals, especially cats. Tell me what I need to do."

"Nothing. They will either take to you or not."

"What in the hell am I supposed to do for a month? I have a business to run." The tone of his voice deepened. "This is not a game to me."

Marty wished she could help him. She gave him an understanding nod. "It will all work out. These things always do," she said in a light voice. "Now, let me show you around the house. Maybe some of the other cats will come out to meet you."

Jeremy set his jaw, pressing his lips into a line and followed her into the room off the foyer.

***

His first impression of the house's interior had been positive. The high ceilings and tall walls of the foyer had been painted white with white wainscoting panels, giving it a clean, crisp feel, especially in the sunshine. However, the living room gave a totally opposite impression. The yellow walls were bright, with the sunlight streaming through tall windows, but the overstuffed sofas, chairs, and ottomans—upholstered in a yellow and red flower pattern—made the room feel busy and cramped. The ornate Oriental rug also contributed to the room's fussy nature, as did all the knickknacks setting on mahogany end tables. It had the look of an old lady's house, which of course it was.

The gray cat had followed them into the living room and continued its leg rubbing routine. Jeremy clenched his teeth, forcing himself not to kick the animal off his pant leg. This was his best Armani suit, for crying out loud. He didn't want cat hair on it.

"Is it true you talk to cats?" Jeremy asked. He wasn't sure how he felt about Marty. She was certainly attractive enough—slender, almost willowy, with a flowing tangle of hair, glinting gold and red in the sunlight. She was, perhaps, dressed a little too casually to meet the new master of the house, but that, of course, was only his opinion. Although he did like the way her cut-off jeans showed her shapely legs and cute little behind. But talking to cats? Come on now. Who'd believe that?

"I communicate with them non-verbally," Marty replied. "Through pictures I see in my head and the feelings I sense."

"Can you tell this one not to rub on my leg?"

He watched the rise and fall of her breasts under her purple, cotton T-shirt. He hoped he wasn't leering, but, damn, she was fine. It had been a while since he last appreciated a woman's breasts. He must be digging out from under Lauren's betrayal, if he could appreciate the view from here.

The sound of the purring cat broke the sudden silence.

Marty reached down and scooped the cat off the carpet. She snuggled it in her arms and gave the top of its head a kiss. She didn't comment, but the look in her green eyes spoke volumes. He'd made another *faux pas*. Get it? *Paw?*

That he could find the tiniest bit of humor in the moment was amazing.

Right then and there, Jeremy resolved to do better. He had to. No matter what she said, Marty held all the power. Over him. His future. She *could* influence these cats. She could talk to them, for Pete's sake. He must try harder to overcome his natural dislike of animals in general, cats in particular.

He put a smile on his face. "I'm sorry. What did you say the cat's name was?"

"Tinkerbelle."

He reached out and stroked the gray head. "Nice to

meet you, Tinkerbelle."

The cat dipped its head to accept the scratch behind her ears.

"Tink says she will try not to rub on your fancy pants."

"I appreciate that." His gaze connected with Marty's.

His sixth sense told him she wasn't fooled by his sudden change of heart. She didn't trust him, just as he didn't trust her...or Ms. Addie's six f-ing cats.

Chapter Three

Ms. Addie's great-nephew didn't believe her. Marty could tell by the strained look on his face. That was all right. She was used to people not believing in her and her gift. In fact, that was one reason she'd taken the job with Ms. Addie. Her benefactress had understood and loved her, more so than even her own family.

Breaking eye contact, Marty turned and started toward the dining room. "Let me show you the rest of the house."

"Please," Jeremy said, "since this is going to be my home for a month."

The insincerity of his tone of voice grated on her. She offered a false weak smile of her own. "This, of course, is the dining room."

They passed through the formal room with its cherry dining table and chairs and built-in china cabinet filled with Ms. Addie's antique, porcelain dinnerware and walked into the kitchen. It also had cherry cabinets and even a refrigerator paneled in the same wood. The countertops were dark green Corian and the floor white marble. Ms. Addie had had a thing for green and white, as well as red as evidenced by the hues of the many roses in her garden.

Marty's chest ached with sadness. Ms. Addie had loved Marty's hair for its red color and its thickness. Many times the gentle lady had lamented the disadvantages of old age, one of them being the thinning of her own hair. She hadn't minded letting herself go gray over the years, saying it looked distinguished, but she'd hated when strands of it came out in her hairbrush.

"I assume those belong to the cats." Jeremy's deep voice cut through Marty's reflection.

She turned her attention to his index finger and followed the direction of his point. Beneath the edge of the center island were six bowls on six placemats, each with the different name printed on it. Letting Tinkerbelle slip from her arms, Marty dropped the cat to the floor where the longhaired feline scampered away.

"Yes, we feed moist food at six o'clock. If a cat doesn't show up, then there is always plenty of dry food." It was her turn to point to the end of another counter, the one nearest the French doors leading to the outside wraparound porch, where a dispenser of dry cat food was located.

"I see," Jeremy said.

A water fountain providing 360-degree access and continuous recirculation of water sat next to the dry food container. "Last year when a few of the cats weren't drinking enough water, I suggested a fountain," Marty explained.

"It seems the cats are well cared for." His tone was cool, dispassionate.

Of course they are! That's my job.

Marty nodded, but tightly, holding back her anger. She'd like to tell this guy to come down off his high horse. She knew he didn't want to be here anymore than she did.

But she had a job to do, and she damn well wasn't going to let his city-slicker high-handedness interfere with her duty to the most wonderful woman she'd ever known.

"I suppose you'll want to learn to feed them," Marty said to him with a sly smirk. She was very pleased with herself when he scowled in return.

But Jeremy recovered nicely, dang him, and agreed. "I suspect that's part of the deal. I'll be happy for you to teach me the ropes."

"Good." She marched out of the side door. "Follow me then," she said over her shoulder. "You might as well learn it all."

The door led to the foyer, but near the back of the house. Marty opened a rear door to reveal a large laundry room that served also as a mudroom. There were two doors at the far end, one with a swinging pet door. The room was well equipped with a washer and dryer, a laundry sink, and various storage cabinets.

"That door leads to the garage." Marty pointed to the door on the south wall. "And the other one opens out to the rose garden."

"Okay."

"And here are the cat pans." She stepped back, and with a wave of her hand, showed him a row of three, high-top litter boxes. Then she opened a low cabinet door. "And here is the bag of litter and the scoop."

"Oh."

She'd flummoxed him now. Marty hid her grin. She

doubted he would like scooping poop, but for the house cats, it was a necessity.

"It must be done twice a day," she informed him.

His laughter was dismissive. "You don't expect me to do that, do you?"

"It's part of the deal." Returning a sweet smile, Marty looked him in the eyes. "And you just agreed to learn it all."

He blew out a noisy breath. "I did, didn't I?

Marty had no sympathy for him, but he sure looked cute standing there with a pinched expression on his bearded face. She wondered if the guy had ever held a cat, or any animal, for that matter. But it wasn't a problem she needed to worry over. Ms. Addie's cats would take care of the introductions themselves. Even though she'd warned them to be nice, Marty knew some of them would push as hard as they could push just to test their new owner.

***

She expected him to clean litter pans? His day was going from bad to worse…and quickly.

Jeremy pressed his lips together and followed Marty from the laundry room back into the foyer. His footfalls echoed on the shiny pine floors, but Marty's bare feet made no sound. She moved as gracefully as the cat that had thankfully disappeared from sight.

"You've seen the downstairs except for the rose garden." Marty turned to glance at him. "I'll show you the upstairs."

He didn't reply but followed her up the staircase with its polished wood banisters and white balusters, eyeing the sway of her behind and the flex of her calf muscles. He topped the last step. A door opened at the head of the stairs and to his left. Jeremy looked to the right to see other open doors, the sunlight shining through them onto the wooden floor of the upstairs foyer.

"We have five full bedrooms and five full baths up here," Marty said as if she was guiding a tour. "I think you might want to use this room as an office. It was Mr. Bynum's years ago."

His "office" was the second door past the staircase landing. He glanced in to see a room, decidedly masculine, painted dark forest green with white trim. Beneath the white chair rail, the walls were wallpapered in a green and white-checkered pattern. Built-in cherry cabinets took up one wall and a large executive desk took up the floor space. A five-story cat condo blocked the view from the window.

The top of the desk was empty except for a longhaired, tri-colored calico cat stretched out in the center, preening herself. A tiny pink tongue licked a white paw in a leisurely manner. The cat didn't even look up to greet them.

"This is Calliope," Marty said.

"Okay." What was he supposed to do? Jump for joy at the introduction?

"She's our princess."

The cat looked like a princess reclining on a throne. With her laid-back attitude, she might not be annoying like that first one. Jeremy glanced down at his trouser legs and noticed streaks of light gray fur glued to his ankles.

At least he could use this green room for work. He'd set up his laptop, after moving the cat from the desk, of course. Maybe he could handle things for a month here. Maybe it would be all right.

Marty turned and crossed the hall. He followed.

"These doors lead to a balcony." She pointed to two solid doors at the end of the hall flanked by tall, skinny windows. "And this is the master bedroom. You can stay in it."

The master bedroom also had a fireplace, but unlike the office, the bedroom had a feminine feel. Below the chair rail, the walls were painted pristine white, a *"color,"* as he was coming to understand, that was a favorite in the house. Wallpaper hung on the walls above the chair rail. The pattern was made up of brownish swirls At least the design wasn't harsh green or bright yellow. But so much white? *Hell.* It was monotonous.

He scowled at the four-poster bed covered in white bed linen and topped with five plump white pillows. It was set in a window alcove. Even though plantation shutters masked the tall windows, silvery light still filtered through.

Marty must have seen his frown because she commented, "After Mr. Bynum died, Ms. Addie preferred to stay in a room down the hall."

He turned to glance at her. Marty's eyes were a little weepy. He'd forgotten she'd lived with Ms. Addie for several years. Of course, she was more torn up by his aunt's death than he was.

When he didn't say anything, she continued. "They were Legend's true romance, Ms. Addie and her husband Roger. A small-town girl meeting a prominent journalist and businessman in the big city of Chicago and bringing him home to Legend. It was very sweet, actually."

Jeremy couldn't imagine romance being sweet, especially since his *true love* had done him dirty and was now married to another man. He should have known never to believe in love and relationships after his mom had done the same thing to his dad.

He felt he needed to say something because she was obviously so taken by the romantic notion. "That's nice." Better to be noncommittal than to voice his actual opinion.

"Yes." She ducked her head, severing eye contact. "That's it for now. The tour that is. You can bring in your luggage or whatever."

"You don't seem to understand," he cut her off, trying hard not to grind his teeth in anger. "I have no luggage because I didn't plan to stay in this town and certainly not under these circumstances."

Her head whipped up. Her expression was pinched, filled with tension, but then she relaxed it as if trying to remain calm. She didn't say anything, but he didn't have to be psychic to read her thoughts. They'd already gone over his motivation downstairs. There was no point in covering old ground.

"Does this town have a clothing store?"

"This town is called Legend," she replied in a snarky tone. "The outlet malls in Pigeon Forge are the closest places where you will find true clothing stores. We have a shop on Main Street that sells clothes to tourists."

"Fine." He could be curt too. "Tell me the name of the store."

"Happy Rags," she said.

Jeremy drew out his iPhone to plug in the name on his notepad. *Great!* He only had one bar. He switched to his settings and looked for a Wi-Fi signal. Nothing. He squeezed his eyes shut while a heavy feeling of dread dropped into his stomach. How in the hell was he supposed to keep his business afloat when he couldn't contact his office? "There's no Wi-Fi."

"What?"

"Internet access." Jeremy opened his eyes and connected to Marty's gaze, reading the confusion in her eyes. "Unless you have a cable connection."

She shook her head. "Ms. Addie didn't have any kind of television. Didn't believe in it. She preferred to spend time with her cats or in the garden with her roses. She also did quite a bit of charity work."

In his mind, he slapped his forehead with the palm of his hand.

Good grief!

What was he going to do now?

"I suppose you don't know if there are any hotspots in town where I can get Wi-Fi connection."

"Well, sure," she said, as if irritated by his assumption

of her ignorance. "Sydney's Coffee Shop has some sort of Internet. I see people in there all the time with laptops."

"Good enough for me." He really had to contact work and check his email, and he couldn't do it isolated on the top of this hill communing with an old lady's cats and their unusual caretaker. Although extremely attractive, the caretaker was turning out to be extremely odd or maybe just extremely naïve.

Marty stepped aside and let him leave the master bedroom.

"I've got to check in with work," he told her, not expecting her to understand the urgency.

She followed him, and now he heard the padding of her feet on the wooden floor hurrying to catch up with him. "Will you be back for the cats' dinner?" she asked.

He rolled his eyes in annoyance, hoping she couldn't see his body language from behind his back.

"I have beef stew in a crockpot for us," she said.

He stopped and turned. "You're providing dinner?" So that was the heavenly aroma he'd smelled in the kitchen when they'd walked through. "I thought I'd grab something while I was in town."

"Oh, no! Ms. Addie was a stickler for eating dinner together," Marty responded. "She thought of a dinner table as a train station platform where you evaluate your day while waiting for the next train. You think about where you've been that day and where you're going the next, and you share your thoughts and feelings with those around the table."

She paused and glanced up at him, her big green eyes expressive, pooling with sadness. As much as he considered her peculiar, at that moment the urge to reach out to her, forget about the pressures of his business, and sit down at that dinner table with her was nearly overpowering.

"It's been a little lonely these past few months at dinnertime without Ms. Addie," she admitted.

Jeremy shook himself mentally. He absolutely, positively would not go soft around this woman. He'd been there and done that. No point in repeating his and his father's mistakes.

"So the cats aren't much company?" He could be snarky too. After all, she'd been portrayed to him as an animal communicator. Didn't the cats converse with her at dinner?

Marty's eyes hardened. "Do what you want. I feed the cats at six o'clock and sit down to dinner myself after that. There will be plenty for you should you choose to join me."

She turned on her heel and stalked up the stairs to the third floor, a place where he had not been invited to tour.

Jeremy shrugged, focusing on the problem at hand—his lack of modern communication ability and his business running without him two hundred miles away. Once the Wi-Fi problem was solved, he knew he could knock out four weeks at Ms. Addie's house. From what he'd seen, getting along with the bunch of felines should be a piece of cake.

He wasn't so sure about their guardian.

Chapter Four

Sydney's Sugar High Coffee Shop and Bakery located across the street from the library faced Main Street. It had Wi-Fi. That's all Jeremy cared about. He sank into one of the sturdy wooden chairs behind a table for two and opened his Mac. The Internet service connected right away, and he was soon checking email and receiving instant messages from his secretary Patsy.

The coffee shop had a homespun feel, kind of Southern and folksy. The atmosphere was welcoming and warm, and the aromas that filled the store made his stomach growl. He hadn't taken time to eat lunch.

"New in town?" an attractive blonde paused at his table and asked.

"Yes," he replied, looking up. The embroidery on the front of her apron read "Sydney," and she wore a gold wedding band on the ring finger of her left hand. Subconsciously, he relaxed, knowing the woman was already taken and wouldn't come onto him as so many single women had the habit of doing.

"Glad to have you in Legend." Her smile was friendly and genuine. "I hope you enjoy your stay. Can I get you anything?"

"Cup of coffee." He glanced back at his laptop. "And I need to borrow some Wi-Fi."

"That's why we have it for the convenience of our

customers."

She left him alone then, and Jeremy went back to IM-ing with a confused Patsy. Figuring he could better explain over the phone, he pressed her name on his iPhone screen, glancing around at the empty shop. Unlikely that he'd be heard, but he still spoke softly as he explained the events of the day to his "*Girl Friday.*"

"That's crazy," Patsy complained. "That's the strangest thing I've ever heard."

"Me too. But if I want the money, I have to stick it out."

"Okay. We'll just make do."

"We have to."

"Don't worry, boss. I can take care of things on my end. You just check in when you can and make friends with those darn cats as quickly as possible."

"I plan on doing just that."

When he pressed the screen to end the conversation, Sydney appeared carrying a coffee in a white porcelain mug and a plate of pastries. It was as if she didn't want to intrude upon his conversation and was waiting for it to end.

Glancing up, Jeremy declined the food. "I didn't order that," he said.

"It's on the house," she told him with another bright smile. "You're a guest in our town. Besides, everyone needs to taste my award-winning scones."

She left him alone then, respecting his privacy. Jeremy devoured the three blueberry scones in record time while he cleaned up his email and made decisions about attendance at an upcoming job fair.

He had Googled "cat behavior" and was reading an Internet article on the subject when two policemen came in and sat down at the table beside him. He glanced up and read Matt Branson and Chris Marks on their uniform nametags. Sydney came over bringing two steaming mugs of coffee and placed them on their table.

"What will it be, boys?" She winked at the policemen.

"You know the usual, Sydney," one replied.

"Comin' your way." She left to go behind the glass-fronted counter packed with bakery goods.

The men looked over at Jeremy and their gazes connected with his.

"New in town?" the one named Chris asked.

Ring up another thing that aggravated him about small towns. Like the store proprietor, the town's finest knew everyone who belonged and those who didn't, and Jeremy guessed they knew all about everyone's business too. Might as well get the introductions over with. He had a month to stick it out here.

"I'm Jeremy Hamilton. Adeline Bynum was my great-aunt."

His name explained everything to the two men, who nodded. "We're sorry about your loss," Matt said. "Ms. Addie was a fine lady. She contributed a lot to our community."

Jeremy acknowledged them with a nod of his own. "So I heard."

The cops sipped their coffee, and Jeremy took a sip of his. Guys weren't much into making idle chat. They weren't going to butt in anymore after he'd identified himself. Jeremy logged off and closed his laptop. He stuck it back into his shoulder bag. He still had to go to Happy Rags and find some casual clothing and a change or two of boxers. He planned on making a stop at the Piggly Wiggly for the toiletries he had not brought with him.

Coming down to the coffee shop every day was going to be inconvenient. Plus, he needed to be making up to those stupid cats. If his work kept him away from the house for long, there would be no way to accomplish his main goal.

He turned to the policemen. "Can you give me some advice?" he asked.

They glanced at him. "Sure. Shoot," Chris said with a wry grin.

"Ms. Addie has no Wi-Fi up at her place. I really need to get some installed." He cleared his throat. "You see, I'll be in town a while."

"Sure thing." Chris glanced at Matt for confirmation. "Donny Fields is the local technician for our regional cable company."

"He owns the electronics repair shop and video store on South Park Street," Matt explained. "It's after four on Friday. I expect he's gone home, but you can call him on

Monday."

Jeremy stood up, feeling for the first time that he had a plan of action and a smidgeon of control over today's events. "Thank you, gentlemen," he said. "You've been a big help."

"See you around?" Matt asked.

"I expect you will," Jeremy replied, his gaze sweeping around the coffee shop and bakery. "I believe this place is going to become one of my favorite places."

***

Marty's head filled with the chatter of five hungry felines that congregated around her feet. As usual when she listened in on their conversations, her heart thrummed with warmth. Even though she was using telepathy to hear them, it was as if that's how they communicated.

Heart-to-heart she liked to think of it.

She'd heard animals talking all her life. It didn't seem strange to her—the happy chatter of a squirrel in a tree or the angry rant of a robin protecting its nest from a cat. She heard them all, but it had taken time and practice to sort them out, to be able to turn them off when she didn't want to hear them, and to figure out how to talk back.

Her ability made her seem odd to most people. Marty understood that. And their contempt made her sad. Her father was a hard man and thought she was crazy. Her mother, used to pleasing her husband, sided with him, so Marty had learned to stifle her gift. It was only after Ms. Addie's encouragement she had been able to accept it. Cherish it. Use it.

Yet, part of her was not ready to do more with her skills. Ms. Addie had urged her to go public, advertise, and make a living from giving readings. Marty had not been able to bring herself to do that. To throw herself open to the ridicule of others was more than she could face. Heck, she'd not even been able to make herself leave the safety of Ms. Addie's house even after the generous woman's death.

"Okay, be patient," she said aloud, but sent an image from her heart for the cats to wait a minute. The logistics of feeding the whole bunch was often difficult. Tonight she was thirty minutes late because she'd hoped Jeremy would show.

"What do you think we'll have tonight for din-din?" Tinkerbelle asked, following Marty to the sink where she washed all six bowls.

"Stop being so eager," Calliope, the calico, retorted and then continued grooming the silky fur on her long, black tail. "You'll get your dinner as usual."

"I hope we have lamb," Gloria commented, trying to cover Calliope's rude remark. "It's much easier on my stomach." Gloria was the oldest cat in the house, a tortoiseshell in color—reddish orange and black—with a distinctive orange stripe down the bridge of her nose.

Jinx, the sleek black cat prowled the perimeter of the kitchen as if he couldn't stay in one place for long. He didn't say anything but glanced at his female companions with contempt.

The last cat in the room, an orange male tabby named Clio, sat next to the water fountain watching the other cats in the room with a worried gaze. "Be nice," he

34

admonished. "Marty is doing her best."

"What do you think of the new guy?" Tinkerbelle asked, following Marty to the refrigerator.

Marty's sixth sense perked up at the question, anxious to hear the response. She removed the plastic container of raw lamb medallions from the refrigerator and returned to the sink.

"How do I know?" Calliope answered the question with another question, her expression bored.

"I watched him from under the bed," Clio admitted. "He seems the nervous type."

An ironic admission from Clio, Marty thought, since he was the most anxious of all Ms. Addie's rescued cats.

Ms. Addie had always fed a good quality kibble to her cats, but once a brand of frozen, raw cat food came on the market, she had added that to the dinner meal on Marty's recommendation. Cats naturally ate whole mice and insects. Most carnivores didn't get enough protein from processed food alone. Now each morning, Marty removed frozen medallions from the freezer bag and placed them in a plastic container to thaw in the refrigerator all day.

"Here ya go, gang." Marty balanced five bowls in her hands and carried them to the island.

One by one, she placed the bowls down on the individual placemats. Tinkerbelle and Gloria were first to their places. Calliope rose and nonchalantly sauntered to her bowl, giving Tinkerbelle a hiss for good measure when she arrived. Jinx silently crept to his place, and finally, after everyone was settled, Clio found his spot. Marty loved watching the furry feline bodies, heads dropped in the bowls gobbling up the raw meat—each different colored tail stretched out straight behind them, sometimes twitching, sometimes quiet and still.

She wished Jeremy was here to see them together like this. One was missing, but that wasn't unusual. Attila marched to the beat of his own drum. The twenty-pound Maine coon was a forceful presence when his lordship decided to favor the household with it.

Lips pressing tight, Marty returned to the sink to wash up. She wasn't surprised Jeremy hadn't returned to the house in time for dinner. This wasn't his decision to stay for a month. Ms. Addie, God rest her soul, had tricked him into it. Even though ill, she'd wanted her money to continue to do good after her death, but Marty couldn't quite see her motive for making the good-looking businessman endure four long weeks with the six cats—and with her.

Marty had just poured herself a glass of red wine when she heard the rumble of the opening garage door. Earlier she'd given Jeremy an opener. Turning, glass in hand, she waited, watching the door. Her heart quickened in anticipation. She heard the opening and shutting of the mudroom door and his footfalls on the wooden floor.

"Sorry I'm late," he announced coming into the kitchen, his arms full of packages. He had removed his coat and tie. His white shirt was opened at the throat.

For a moment, time stopped—and then whisked ahead in a dreamlike, imaginary swiftness. Marty's nerve endings tingled with awareness, and she grew light-headed. She had a vivid picture of this same thing happening again, in this same place, at the same time, only years from now. Not déjà vu, but a precognition, a foretelling of things to come. Then as the scene shifted, her body flooded with warmth, and she saw this ruggedly handsome man in the most intimate way. They were sexual partners. Happily married. In love.

Marty's face flushed hot. She turned quickly to avoid his gaze and put down her wine glass. "I'm glad you made it. Have you eaten? I'm just sitting down myself."

"Sydney fed me a while ago, but I'm still hungry."

She felt him move from behind, coming toward her while she reached to remove another glass and bowl from the upper cabinet. She stilled. Every fiber of her being vibrated with acute awareness and the sense it was meant to be. Would he kiss her? It would happen. It was expected.

"I bought French bread at the coffee shop," Jeremy said. "I thought it sounded good with beef stew."

Marty glanced at the proffered package of French bread wrapped in white paper. Her imaginary balloon suddenly deflated, she took the package from him. "Thanks. Have a seat."

He dropped the other bags on the top of the island and watched the five cats cleaning whiskers and paws, ignoring him as if he were invisible.

"I guess they've eaten."

"It doesn't take them long to finish," she told him, trying to ignore her own feeling of inevitability. "If they don't, then another cat will take their food."

"There are sure a lot of them." His comment sounded as if he was overwhelmed.

"They are all here but one." She laid his place setting—napkin, fork, spoon, knife. She brought butter from the refrigerator and put it on the table.

She would do this again. Sometime in the future. Her sixth sense was filling her with a strange premonition. At the same time, her nerves came alive, and she felt nauseous. A fluttery feeling of butterflies in her stomach made her want to throw up. Instead, she sipped some wine, hoping it would calm her.

Jeremy sat down. "They don't seem to notice me. I thought they'd be all over me, like this afternoon when I first came in."

"Oh, they notice you," Marty said. "They're trying to act nonchalant."

"Independent," he offered.

She looked at him. "They were talking about you earlier."

Jeremy rolled his eyes.

Marty flushed when she saw him trying to bite back a grin. Obviously, he thought she was a nut. *Good grief.* What was wrong with her? What made her think she and Jeremy would someday be together? What would he ever see in her?

Seriously, why was she doing this to herself? She understood how lonely she'd always been and how she'd dreamed of a "sweet someone" to sweep her off her feet and make her life better. But she knew that to be a pipedream. Only she had the power to make herself happy. No man, no person had that control.

She wouldn't give him that control, for one thing. She wouldn't be like her mother, always wanting to please a man. Ms. Addie had shown her the way to be her own woman. She'd loved Mr. Bynum, but they were partners, not co-dependents. Ms. Addie had been a strong woman, no matter how frail physically at the end, with a mind of her own. Marty would be like her. That was her dream.

Not some psychic-like vision of Jeremy Hamilton sweeping her off her feet and into a life of wedded bliss.

Chapter Five

They ate dinner together, like an old married couple, and drank several glasses of pinot noir. Then they'd cleaned the kitchen, sharing the washing and drying chores because there weren't enough dishes to put in the dishwasher. After that, they'd looked at each other awkwardly.

Jeremy wasn't sure what was expected of him. He had loaded up on allergy medicine so felt fairly confident he could get up close and personal with the fur balls without succumbing to respiratory distress. He had psyched himself into petting a cat or two after his meal, but they all vanished as soon as they finished grooming. With the cats gone and the July evening warm, Marty suggested they sit in the garden a while.

"I'd better put my new clothes away," Jeremy said. Uneasiness motivated him to break off their time together. The little dinner party seemed too intimate in a non-sexual way, but at the same time, he had this unexplainable notion he'd like to take his new companion to bed.

There was no way he was going to act on those impulses. Aunt Addie would probably thunderbolt him into the ground. Better to excuse himself and head up to his room with his packages.

"Here," Marty said, handing him a lint roller advertised for "*pet hair removal.*" "I thought you might need this."

He looked at her with a questioning gaze.

She nodded toward his trouser legs. "For your pants. You know, because of Tinkerbelle."

Jeremy glanced down, remembering the affectionate cat from earlier in the afternoon. "Thanks."

Taking the roller brush from her hands, his gaze lingered a little too long on her lips. She certainly looked kissable enough with her hair fluffed out around her face like a halo and cat hair coating her T-shirt. *Good grief!* Some of that cat hair must be coating his brain if he thought rolling around with a be-furred nut case sounded good. He better get the hell out of Dodge before he found himself doing more than making nice with a bunch of cats. He picked up his bags, gave her a tight-lipped smile, and escaped to the sanctuary of the pristine master bedroom.

The day had been a long one—the drive from Louisville through the mountains, the bad news from the lawyer, and the meeting with Marty. And the cats. He couldn't forget the cats. He'd met them all except one, but had failed to form much of an impression. Tinkerbelle was annoying with her constant rubbing. Calliope seemed aloof and not an issue. The rest? Who knew? He certainly wasn't going to dwell on them tonight. Maybe tomorrow when he was rested he'd be better able to formulate a plan of how he was going to cozy up to the half-dozen felines.

He fell into a deep sleep in the comfortable four-poster bed.

Sometime in the night, his dreams became vivid, full of flashes of red hair and the whisperings of lovemaking. His crotch was warm, radiating the heat of an erection. Tender love nips caressed his cheeks. He groaned aloud, living in the erotic moment complete with vibrator and tickling sex toys. In his dream, Marty was there, covering his mouth with kisses and whispering of love. He reached out to her and froze when he touched…fur?

Jeremy's eyes flew open.

What the hell?

Over his head a cat face, complete with white whiskers and an orange stripe down the bridge of its nose, loomed over him.

He remained quiet, afraid to move for fear the cat would scratch his eyes out. The thing vibrated, purring loudly. It put its paw on his shoulder and grazed his cheek with sharp, little teeth. Jeremy swallowed carefully. Glancing down at his legs, he saw the orange cat curled up right on his crotch, sleeping soundly.

"Go away," he said softly. "Please go away."

Instead, the dark cat curled up near his neck, continuing the annoying purr. He felt his eyes begin to water and itch. Yet, he couldn't move. Could hardly breathe. What if the cat on his legs maimed his groin and genitals in a horrific way? He had heard of the damage a cat scratch could do. Jeremy lay flat on his back, his sexy dream transformed into a nightmare of major proportions. Somehow he passed the night in a state of abject horror.

When he awoke, his bed was empty. The only indication of his terrifying night was a small indention on his pillow and a telltale fluff of cat fur.

Jeremy sat up in bed and, leaning forward, scraped his

fingers through his hair. Cats had made themselves at home in his bed. For crying out loud! But what about the dream? Why had Marty been part of it? The cats, of course...and her connection to them. The brain played funny tricks. This was one of them, especially since his acceptance by the cats and their guardian was so critical to his company's future.

That was it. The dream had nothing to do with the real person—Marty with her sexy legs and darling butt and billowing red hair. No, it had nothing to do with a passing attraction that he had no intention of acting on.

Jeremy flung the white covers back and rose from bed. Naked except for a pair of blue boxers, he padded to the bathroom. He needed a shower. A long hot one first, and then a cold finisher to chase away the lust-filled remnants of that creepy dream.

He didn't care for the en suite that adjoined the master bedroom. It was long and narrow with white tile, of course, and the shower wasn't a real shower, but an old-fashioned claw-foot tub made of cast iron and lined with porcelain. The door didn't really shut properly either, like the house had settled and the latch didn't properly engage. He pulled it shut and hoped it would stay closed while he was in the shower.

The white, antique tub had been fitted with a shower enclosure with a showerhead mounted at one end. A thin, white curtain hung from a rod that circled the tub.

Stepping into the tub was awkward because of its height. The shower curtain hooks rattled on the rod loud enough to wake the dead when Jeremy pulled it around to enclose the tub. He felt cramped. He was too big for the space. Too tall. Too wide. The claw-foot tub needed the body of a dainty woman in it, lounging back in a soapy bubble bath, her red hair dangling down her back.

He pushed the sudden vision of Marty aside as he scrubbed himself clean with soap that lathered well but smelled of roses. He made sure the water was hot for the first pass. The hotter the better. Steam filled the bathroom.

And then he turned off the hot, leaving a cold downpour of water for just a few seconds. Shivering and invigorated, he turned off the faucet and yanked back the shower curtain.

"Hiss!"

"What the hell?"

Jeremy swiped water out of his eyes with the back of a hand. He blinked once. Twice. It couldn't be. A miniature lion with paws the size of ham hocks splayed out on the side of the tub.

The monster hissed again, baring huge white fangs, and then lifted a fat paw, claws extended, and slapped it against Jeremy's hairy, wet leg.

"Ahhhhhhhhhhhhhhhh!" The stinging was instant and intense. Jeremy recoiled and stumbled backward. He grabbed the flimsy shower curtain. The plastic shower hooks snapped like rifle shots and the curtain ripped from the rod.

Arms flapping for control, Jeremy slid on his butt and hit his head on the back of the tub with a sharp whack. The shower curtain tangled around his legs making it impossible

44

for him to regain his footing. He lay on the floor of the tub, catching his breath.

What the hell was that? He peeked over the side of the tub but couldn't see anything. Whatever that animal was, it had disappeared. The bathroom door was cracked though. "Damn!" he cursed. "Damn, damn, damn!"

He would murder that creature. He'd make it pay for scaring the shit out of him. Casting off the shower curtain, Jeremy fought to turn himself over in the tub and braced with his hands to get his body into a crawling position. Then he pushed his butt in the air preparing to stand just as the bathroom door flew open.

"Jeremy, are you okay?" Marty cried, racing into the room.

Just great. What in the hell else could go wrong today? He climbed to his feet and turned toward Marty. She stood in the middle of the floor staring at him. Her face was as red as her hair, and her mouth was as wide as a chasm.

***

"Oh, my!"

Marty whipped around to face the door wanting to look anywhere but at the stark naked man standing in Miss Addie's tub. *Please God, let the floor open up and swallow me whole.* She'd never been so embarrassed in her life. But it wasn't her fault she'd come busting into the bathroom unannounced. Jeremy had screamed like a girl. For all she knew, he was being murdered. And how was she to know he was in the shower? In his birthday suit. And what was up with that? Why didn't he cover up? Couldn't he tell she was uncomfortable?

"Are you okay? Can I get you something?"

"A towel."

Marty stood rooted in the spot. A towel? Oh, sure. She'd have to turn and look at him again. She'd never seen a naked man. At twenty-one she was particularly naïve, she knew. But she'd never dated. Men didn't flock to women they thought crazy. Communicating with animals put her in that category.

Marty licked her lips. Okay, she could do this. She turned slowly, averting her gaze.

"A towel," she murmured.

The white terrycloth bath towel hung a few feet away on a rack. Why was Jeremy incapable of moving from the tub to reach it? She heard him taking deep breaths. Maybe to steady his nerves. She was the one who needed hers steadied. She slid along the floor, trying not to look at him and keeping the towel in her focus.

She snatched it from the rack and, with her hand outstretched, side-walked toward the tub.

"Thanks." His voice was flat.

"Sure thing."

Now get me out of here!

Marty let go of the towel before it was securely in Jeremy's grasp. It dropped like a rock to the floor.

"Oh, no!"

She stooped to scoop the towel off the white tiles, and

as she stood, she couldn't help but glance upward. Jeremy wasn't a big man, but he *was* well endowed. Big time. Or so it seemed to her from her precarious position on the floor looking up. Too late his hands moved to shield his groin.

Her breath abandoned her. She was stuck in the reality of the moment, her cheeks and neck red hot with humiliation and the rest of her body warm with another strange feeling.

"Ah, sorry. Here ya go."

He yanked the towel from her hands and wrapped it around his waist so that the terry cloth hid the object foremost in her mind.

"What's the matter?" He met her gaze with a frown. "Have you never seen a man naked?"

"Ah, not lately." That wasn't entirely a lie. Not lately was almost the same as never.

"A woman as pretty as you?"

"Ms. Addie ran a tight ship. She didn't allow cavorting in the house." Let him think she didn't bring her men friends home out of respect for Ms. Addie's rules. She'd be damned if she'd let him think no one wanted to date her. Better he thought her a little wild than a big failure.

Her parents had been the ones who had kept the tight ship, ashamed of a daughter they thought weird. Their embarrassment had rubbed off on her as a kid, so she'd failed to make many friends or date. She'd grown to prefer the unconditional love of animals to that of unpredictable, selfish, and sometimes greedy humans.

She dropped her gaze again unable to meet his just in case he could see she was lying. "You're hurt."

He glanced down and saw the blood trickling down his shin. "I think one of your damned cats attacked me. The mountain lion."

"Attila."

This was horrible. She'd warned Attila to be on his best behavior. The Maine coon was the house protector, and he was leery of change. Ms. Addie's death had hit him hard. It was no wonder he'd chosen to claim his territory, not accepting the new owner and threatening him as an intruder.

"Let me clean the wound for you."

"No, it's okay. It just a scratch—well, actually six scratches." He lifted a knee and stepped out of the tub.

"It's not okay." Marty was firm. All she knew about men came from knowing her dad, and he could be stubborn. "Cats can carry bacteria in their claws," she said. "You need your leg cleaned."

Their gazes connected, and it was almost as if Marty could see his mind churning. She guessed he wanted no help from her. He was in a difficult situation having to live here a month, but she was trapped too because of her loyalty to Ms. Addie. Heck, she'd rather be anywhere but Ms. Addie's bathroom with a naked man.

Granted, he was a handsome, naked man. *Still.*

"Suit yourself," Jeremy finally said with a shrug.

"I'll be right back. I need to get my first aid kit."

Marty fled, giving herself time to quiet her fluttering heart. *Dang!* What a way to start the morning.

When Marty returned to the bathroom, she found Jeremy seated on the closed toilet seat. Thankfully, he was wearing boxer shorts.

It still was an intimate situation—too personal for her tastes. Yet, what else could she do but muddle through it? Ms. Addie always said a person gained confidence by facing one's fear. Once done, a person's confidence increased, and having courage was easier the next time.

Without a word, Marty knelt in front of him. He really had the hairiest legs. Forcing down the knot in her throat, she patted his wound with a cotton ball soaked in hydrogen peroxide.

His skin smelled of Ms. Addie's favorite rose soap.

"I hope this doesn't hurt." She couldn't think of anything else to say.

"I can take it."

Sure he could. Yet, she'd heard him cry out like a girl. Big, tough man to be scared of a little cat. Hiding a smile, Marty gently blotted the area dry.

"Maine coon cats are generally big and sturdy. Attila weighs about twenty pounds. That's average for the breed," she told him while patting on antibiotic ointment with a clean cotton ball. "They have large paws as a rule, but you may have noticed Attila's look even bigger."

She traced the outline of the scratched area with a fingertip. "Most cats have five toes on each front paw, but

49

Attila has a genetic abnormality with six toes on each front paw."

Looking up, she found Jeremy watching her with an odd gaze. Hearing his uneven breathing and caressing his skin made Marty's own skin tingle.

She cleared her throat and then continued. "He's called a polydactyl cat. See. You can count the six claw marks."

"Very interesting." He touched the top of her hand to still it. "Yet, it doesn't explain why the beast tried to kill me."

Marty sucked in a breath, lost in Jeremy's blue eyes. "Attila wasn't trying to kill you."

"You could have fooled me."

"It was more of a warning," Marty said. "He doesn't want you around."

Jeremy's eyes narrowed. "Then you tell that damn cat he'd better get used to me. Tell him before the month ends, we're going to be BFFs."

Chapter Six

It wasn't even noon, yet it had already been one helluva day.

Jeremy seethed with the frustration of his situation. To think his fate rested in the hands of a weird cat woman with a shock of red wavy hair and creamy skin that gazed at him in a guarded way. He'd already found himself lost in her eyes one too many times, trying to figure out if she had something between the ears as well as a beautiful body.

Marty was the key to his success, no matter what she said. She knew the contingent of Aunt Addie's damn cats. Knew what made them tick. He needed to tap into her knowledge so he could end this farce as quickly as possible.

Jeremy dressed in a pair of shorts and a dark green and gold football jersey reading "Legend Dragons." He didn't have a pair of casual shoes, something he needed to correct today, so he put on his dirty socks and dress shoes. *Shit!* He must look ridiculous. Or like his grandfather back in the day.

The aroma of coffee met him when he opened his bedroom door and stepped into the hall. He followed the smell down the stairs and into the kitchen and stopped in the doorway. Marty was sitting at the oval table with a newspaper spread in front of her, a mug of coffee in her hands, and the monster cat guarding her ankles.

"Good morning, again," he said.

Marty's gaze lifted, her eyes wide, and then she ducked her head. Maybe she was still embarrassed for seeing him in all his naked glory. Why hadn't he been quicker to cover himself? All women weren't like Lauren who'd often paraded around his condo in the nude. Marty seemed modest, a bit naïve. He should have respected her more.

In a second, she rallied, glanced up, and smiled. "Good morning...again."

Jeremy marched into the kitchen as if the alpha cat wasn't in the room and had never been bested by him. He skirted around the guard cat that hissed at him when he passed.

"Good morning to you too," he said to the creature and got another hiss for his trouble.

"Attila!"

"Never mind," Jeremy said. "He'll come around."

Attila stalked off, his polydactyl paws striking the tile floor with a clipping sound. He was a light brown tabby with a white underbelly and white paws. His coat was shaggy and the fur around his head and cheeks gave him the male lion-like appearance. Attila proudly carried his tail high as if giving Jeremy the finger on his way out the door.

Jeremy mentally reciprocated with the image of his own middle finger.

"Coffee?" Marty asked, starting to rise.

"Stay there." He held up his hand to halt her. "I can get it. Just tell me where to find a mug."

"In the top cabinet over the coffee pot. There's half-

and-half in the fridge. Do you take sugar?"

"No. I drink it black." What was the point of coffee if you defiled it with foo-foo stuff? Even diluting it with some form of milk was a nonstarter for him.

Jeremy found a mug and filled it with coffee from an old-fashioned coffee pot. Then he sat down opposite Marty and took his first sip.

She was dressed in a bright green tank top that nicely showed off the curve of her breasts. He couldn't pull his gaze from them. He hadn't noticed her clothing earlier that morning, being preoccupied by being attacked, but once again she was barefoot and wore blue jean cutoffs, giving testament to her hillbilly persona.

He liked that about her. She seemed natural and unstuffy, unlike Lauren. She seemed gentle. And sure of herself, of this natural ability she had, even though he was unsure about her.

Shoving a section of the paper toward him, Marty said, "The *Legend Post-Dispatch*. Ms. Addie's husband used to own it."

"Really? What happened to it?" Was it part of his inheritance? That was what he actually wanted to know.

"Ms. Addie hired Pete Garrity as managing editor some time ago. Shortly after she died, Pete learned he'd inherited the paper. It's quite a town institution. It would have been a shame to lose it."

"I see," Jeremy said, but he didn't. He guessed the newspaper was part of the "certain items" bequeathed to other people. Ms. Addie, canny old lady, probably knew

Jeremy would sell the paper, and her husband's news organization would be lost to the town.

"Care for some of Sydney's scones or muffins?" Marty lifted a corner of the newspaper and showed him a plate of pastries hiding beneath the newsprint. "I had time earlier to run downtown and pick them up."

He reached for a scone. "Thanks. These things are addictive."

Biting into a scone, he chewed thoughtfully. Marty went back to reading an article. Her right index finger was outstretched, and she was using it as a place marker as she read. Sensing his perusal, she glanced up.

"What?"

"Nothing."

She went back to the paper, and he munched in silence, watching her. Once again he felt the familiarity of this moment, and it unnerved him. He'd never eaten a meal with another woman that felt so casual and relaxed. Nothing was expected of him. Even when he and Lauren were hot and heavy, it was more of a sexual thing. Not something that felt so inexplicably comfortable. He couldn't remember ever sharing dinner or breakfast with Lauren that they weren't either going to bed or thinking about it.

It wasn't that Marty didn't attract him. She did. He'd dreamed about her last night, for God's sake. But that was because some stupid cat was caressing his cheek and another was sleeping on his crotch.

"Why would a cat nip your cheek?" he asked.

Marty met his gaze. "Did you have one do that?"

"Yes."

"Which one?"

"The one with the orange nose."

"Gloria." Marty gave a knowing smile. "She likes you."

Jeremy sat back in his chair and rubbed his jaw. One down, five to go. "That's a good thing," he said.

"Yes," Marty agreed. "Gloria is the oldest cat. She has a lot of influence on the others."

Almost as if thinking about her conjured her up, Gloria arrived in the room walking sedately. She hopped up on an empty chair at the table and watched them with her wide, yellow cat eyes.

***

With Gloria in Jeremy's corner, Marty knew the others would come around. She hoped it would happen before the end of the month. He really needed his inheritance, and she'd like to see him get it.

But where would she go then? She tapped her finger on the newspaper and bit her bottom lip. She was desperate to find answers. Taking care of Ms. Addie's cats and living in the house was part of her agreement. But if Jeremy moved in or wanted to sell the property, what then? How could she put her life on hold for as long as it took the cats to live out their natural lives?

That hadn't been an issue until yesterday. Until Jeremy walked into the house, and Marty realized she wanted more out of life than living alone with a bunch of cats. And if Jeremy lived here, how could she continue to live here too? Not with the odd flutter of her heart every time she looked at him. Not after seeing him naked. Not if he wasn't attracted to her.

Lifting the mug to her lips, Marty sipped the now tepid coffee. Tinkerbelle paraded into the room and rubbed against her legs to say hello. She twirled around Jeremy's bare legs as well. He made an effort to reach down and scratch behind an ear. A loud purr was his reward for effort.

A rap on the French doors interrupted Marty's thoughts and announced the arrival of the gardener Woody. He pushed the doors open, bringing with him a rush of summer air into the cool kitchen.

"Howdy, Ms. Marty," Woody said and glanced at Jeremy. Woody was Marty's age, a lanky, country kid recently out of high school and without many prospects. He took care of Ms. Addie's rose garden and kept the yard cut.

"Morning, Woody. This is Jeremy, Ms. Addie's nephew," she said. "He will eventually own the house."

Jeremy rose and extended his hand. "Nice to meet you."

Woody wiped his hand on his jeans and then reached out to grasp Jeremy's hand. He nodded but didn't say anything. Marty noticed Jeremy's frown as the two shook hands.

Woody ended the handshake quickly, taking a shuffling

step backwards. Then turning to Marty, Woody said, "Guess I'll get started."

"Great," she answered, hoping to cover the awkward moment. "Thanks, as always, for your help."

Woody left through the other kitchen door going toward the mudroom and the back door to the garden. Jeremy continued standing. Marty turned a questioning gaze up to him.

"I guess I'll get started too."

"Okay." What did he plan to do today?

As if reading her mind, he explained, "I'm going to set up my laptop in the office. Even without Wi-Fi, I think I can still do some work. I'll call Monday to get it installed here. Later today, I need to drive to one of the outlet malls for a pair of casual shoes."

She smiled up at him. "I think your fancy shoes look quite charming with your shorts."

He grinned in return. "Thanks, but they don't compliment my football jersey very well. I really need to do something about my wardrobe."

"I can see your point. Those shoes don't do much for the Legend Dragons colors."

Their banter seemed natural. Marty couldn't shake that feeling of ease. Damned oddest thing too. When Jeremy left the room, it felt empty without him.

And the man had only been in Legend one day.

***

"Quiet! Here she comes!"

Marty sensed a conspiracy underfoot the moment she entered the kitchen to find all six cats patiently waiting for dinner.

"Well, the gang's all here," she said aloud and silently communicated a happy image of welcome.

She didn't receive a welcome in return. Not from all of them. Tinkerbelle, of course, was ready for din-din. She always liked to eat. But Calliope was standoffish more than usual, and Clio nervously swished his tail. Jinx crouched under the table watching. Attila felt downright hostile.

Gloria, huddled by the water fountain, moved to stand under Marty's feet as she prepared the nightly dishes of raw medallions—beef this time.

Keeping her senses tuned, Marty picked up on the conversation.

"It's all Gloria's fault," Calliope said. A pout was tangible in his body language.

"Shhhh," Attila warned.

And then they all clammed up. Marty envisioned Jinx's afternoon hunting mice. She saw Calliope preening herself in a sunny window. But whatever the cats were discussing had ceased as soon as she entered the room.

Something was definitely up.

***

Jeremy returned from his trip to Pigeon Forge wearing his new purchases from the outlet mall—a red polo shirt, khaki shorts and real, honest to goodness Nike Free Trainers. He dumped his packages upstairs on his bed and then went back down to the kitchen looking for Marty. The house was eerily quiet. The black cat—Jinx he thought— skirted his feet and slipped silently away with not so much as a flick of a tail.

"Where is everyone?" He stopped a moment and examined the feeling of disappointment that washed over him when he found she wasn't waiting for his return. Funny how he had come to depend on her presence in this house after such a short time

Jeremy searched the house, but it was empty. He wandered out the back door into the garden. A heady aroma of roses assaulted his senses as he walked a stone path between manicured bushes of reds and yellows and whites. In an alcove of shrubs, he found Marty sitting cross-legged on a wooden bench, her eyes shut and the back of her hands resting on her knees, palms up. The flame of the setting sun burnished her hair and illuminated her face.

The serenity of the moment overwhelmed him. Transfixed, he watched. She was beautiful. And calm and peaceful. God, he longed for that same kind of tranquility in his life. Instead, his body was under constant stress, tense from the pressures of his job and the expectations he put on himself. He wished he could project that kind of calmness instead of being so damn uptight.

But who had time to sit around with nothing to do but gaze at the back of eyelids? Not him. There was too much to do to run a successful business. Unlike Marty who seemed to do nothing all day but commune with cats.

He felt like a fool, but he had to say something to get her attention. He lowered his voice to just above a whisper. "What are you doing?"

His question didn't break her mood. She didn't even open an eye. It was almost as if she knew he was standing there.

"Meditating. Come join me."

He took a step toward her. "I don't know how." Suddenly it seemed to be the thing he most wanted to do—to join her, to be a part of whatever she was a part of.

"Just sit down."

He did. Sitting on the stone path beneath his feet, heedless of the dirt smudging his new shorts, he crossed his legs like Marty's, something he hadn't done since elementary school and glanced up at her.

"Now what."

She still hadn't opened her eyes. Hadn't looked at him.

"Shut your eyes. Stop your inner chatter. Open your heart."

All easier said than done. He tried. He really tried, but he kept thinking how stupid this was. What if Patsy saw him? She'd laugh out loud. Lauren too. My God, his ex would have had a conniption fit seeing him like this.

"Am I supposed to say something to get started?"

"Sitting in silence teaches you to listen and connect with your higher self."

"Oh, sure." His higher self was telling him this was

60

crazy. Jeremy opened his eyes. Marty sat there, eyes closed, shoulders relaxed. "How in the hell do you do that?"

She let out a long breath. "Here's a tip. Keep your eyes closed and become aware of your breathing pattern."

"Okay." He shut his eyes again and listened to each inhalation and exhalation, finding it somehow soothing.

"Don't try and control what comes into your head," she said softly. "Focus on nothing. From there you will find your truth."

It sounded like mumbo jumbo, but Jeremy gave it a shot. Slowly, he unwound. The tension lifted from his shoulders.

He didn't find his truth.

Being so near Marty, all he discovered was a heightened awareness of her. And an overpowering desire to take her to bed.

Chapter Seven

Jeremy didn't take Marty to bed, and he made damn sure he didn't take any cats either, locking the bedroom door for good measure. Sleep came swiftly and peacefully.

On Sunday morning, the sunshine of the previous days was missing. And so was any interruption in the shower. No miniature lion, but too bad Marty didn't burst in again. He'd enjoyed her discomfort.

Later, after dressing, he followed the aroma of coffee and bacon into the kitchen to find Marty standing at the stove.

"Good morning."

She turned at his greeting, spatula in hand, and waved it at him. "Good morning. How are you?"

Dressed in a black pencil skirt, flats, and a white, cotton peasant blouse, she looked different. Pretty. Feminine. The way the blouse draped from her shoulders and opened at the neck revealed a creamy expanse of skin—her collarbones and her slender throat. She wore make-up too, a little lipstick and eyeliner, loopy earrings, and a half-dozen gold bracelets on her right wrist. Gone was the hillbilly, replaced by a hippy chick.

"I slept like a baby," he said, strolling across the floor.

She raised a knowing eyebrow. "Meditation."

"Meditation?" Come on, now. Five minutes on his

bum in the dirt with his eyes closed. *I don't think so.* He waved off her assertion with a free hand.

"You were relaxed when you went to bed, weren't you?"

He opened the door to the cabinet where he found a clean mug and poured a steaming cup of coffee. "Sure, but I didn't have any feline night visitors waking me up either."

"I asked them to stay away," she said, placing a plate of crispy bacon on the table.

He picked up a slice and pointed at her. "I also locked the door."

She had no response for his logic. Instead she changed the subject. "I'm going to church this morning. I try to keep Ms. Addie's routines. She would like that. Want to come?"

"I don't do church." He finished his first slice of bacon. "Thanks anyway."

She shrugged as if to say *suit yourself* and wiped her hands on a kitchen towel. "If you want eggs, they're in the fridge."

In other words, you can cook them yourself. Fine with him. He didn't eat much breakfast. Jeremy sat down instead and reached for the Sunday newspaper.

"Okay."

"Oh, I forgot to tell you something last night." Marty turned, licking her lips and smiling as if anticipating his reaction. "I got your Wi-Fi fixed."

"What?" His brain fought to understand what she was telling him. Marty didn't seem the technical type. "How did you do that?"

"Donny Fields is my cousin. While you were gone yesterday, he came over as a favor to me." She grinned at his disbelief. "It's installed all over the house."

He rose, feeling lightheaded at the sudden good news. Now he could get his work done. He wasn't disconnected from his world. "Thank you! I could kiss you for that."

Jeremy caught her upper arms and drew her toward him. The swift kiss was hardly anything to savor. Surprise written in her wide eyes, Marty didn't respond to the pressure of his lips on hers. But he did. His toes tingled in his brand new Nikes. His gut clenched with sharp desire. Damn! What was he doing?

He drew back and dropped his hands. For the first time in his life, he felt awkward after kissing a woman. From the looks of her red, flushed face, Marty was feeling it too. Her mouth formed a little "O" of surprise. In shock, she appeared adorable. Jeremy repressed the urge to kiss her again and turned away.

Strangely, his tongue was now tied. He touched the newspaper for lack of anything else to do with his hands. Where was his assertiveness? His take-charge mentality? It had left him as quickly as he'd kissed Marty.

"Well, I'd better go, or I'll be late."

"Sure." He turned. "Thanks again. I can get some work done today."

She blushed and ducked her head. "No problem. I

64

knew you needed it."

He didn't want her to leave. Stupid, really. She'd be back soon. But for one more moment of having her in his presence, he called her name. "Marty!"

She looked back at him.

"Is everyone in this town someone's cousin?"

She laughed, and it cleared the air. "Just about. It's a small town after all."

***

Marty left before Jeremy thought to ask about the information he needed to access the Wi-Fi. He had a good excuse. Other things had distracted his mind. *Duh.*

After cleaning up the kitchen, he went upstairs to the office, thinking he could get some work done without the Internet, and happily discovered written instructions and the default password for his new Wi-Fi under the laptop. Marty's installer must have left them there. Setting up his MacBook with the Wi-Fi proved to be a breeze, and he was soon logging on and connecting with his work email account.

In the midst of replying to an email from Patsy about her sick dog, Jeremy was interrupted by a thud as the gray cat Tinkerbelle jumped up on the desk.

"Well, hello."

Silently Tinkerbelle glided across the cherry desktop and padded right over his laptop keyboard. "Mmmmmmmmmmm" appeared on the computer screen.

Tinkerbelle turned and sashayed back over the keyboard, swishing a long, fluffy tail in Jeremy's nose. Jeremy swatted it away. His jaw tightened in irritation.

"Hey!" Jeremy cried out in protest.

"Meow," Tinkerbelle responded in a purring voice.

"Meow yourself, you damn cat."

When the gray cat wouldn't leave him alone, Jeremy grabbed her under the belly and dropped her unceremoniously onto the wooden floor. Out of the corner of his eye, he spotted the miniature lion at the office door, poking his head around the corner and staring at him with what Jeremy thought was contempt.

"Stay away, you damn cat," Jeremy said, not even trying to hide his anger.

Then Tinkerbelle swept under the desk between his bare legs and curled around them. Jeremy held his breath. *Damn it!* He couldn't treat these cats as if they were the pieces of crap he thought they were. These animals were his ticket out of the economic mess he faced. He, at least, needed to make an effort.

Before Jeremy could do anything to make amends, Tinkerbelle ran from under the desk, across the floor, and out the door. Attila disappeared from view too. Jeremy sighed and sat back in his chair. Marty was gone. It was a perfect time to befriend the cats. Instead he'd blown it.

Rising from the chair, Jeremy closed the Mac. At a complete loss about where and how to start, he decided to begin with the basics. Marty expected him to clean cat pans. So clean the litter boxes he would.

In the mudroom, he found the scoop and a plastic grocery bag for the poop and clumps of cat litter. Grimacing, he kept the plastic scoop at arm's length as he dug into the three dirty litter boxes. *Ewww!* Sure was smelly. Nevertheless, he finished the chore and went outside into the garage to dispose of the bag of waste in the outside garbage can.

The door was locked when he tried to go back into the house.

"What the…?" Jeremy grabbed the doorknob with both hands and shook it. Had he tripped the lock when he went out? Now what was he to do?

He pushed the button to lift the garage door. It was raining cats and dogs, as the old saying went. Thunder rumbled in the distance. *Wonderful.* Jeremy dashed down the sidewalk through water puddles and onto the covered porch. He tried the French doors at the kitchen. *Locked.* He tried the front doors. *Locked.*

Completely defeated, for Marty had given him a garage door opener to put in his car but no keys to the house, Jeremy slumped into one of the white wooden rocking chairs lining the porch. At least he was out of the pouring rain. He rested his head on the high back and rocked away his frustrations, gazing at the green front lawn that sloped down the hill and thinking he'd like to kill a couple of cats.

***

Marty saw Jeremy sitting on the front porch as she drove up the driveway. She parked her economical Honda Fit and shut the garage door and walked around to the porch. He was asleep. His head drooped to one side, and a wet lock of his brown hair was plastered on his forehead. His mouth was slightly open. Her heart fluttered in her chest. If she overlooked the beard, she could envision him as a child sound asleep in bed. The cuteness factor overwhelmed her, and she smiled.

But then she remembered his sweet kiss. It was an all too vivid memory. She'd been taken aback, totally surprised, and unable to react. Where had the kiss come from? Why hadn't she responded? Dang if she'd admit she'd never been kissed by a man. No, a twenty-first century women never admitted her lack of education.

"Hey." She pushed his shoe with the toe of hers.

He startled awake, his head jerking up. "Good God, you're finally home."

Marty nodded as he actually rubbed the sleep from his eyes, reminding her once again of a little child. But then he stood, towering over her. This man was no child. He was a man full grown. She'd seen that for herself, hadn't she? The thought made her blush, and, as usual, she shifted her gaze to her shoes. Maybe her shyness was her main problem with men. If she was only more assertive, maybe that gratitude kiss she'd received from Jeremy wouldn't be the extent of her experience with men.

"Why are you out here?" She forced herself to lift her eyes up to his.

"I locked myself out of the damn house."

She managed a smile. Suddenly, her surroundings sprang into sharp focus. The dampness of the gloomy day, the distinctive smell of rain, the sound of precipitation hitting the metal roof, and Jeremy's very nearness...his maleness. And she was alone with him.

Marty put distance between them, walking away from him toward the front door because she couldn't handle the sensations bombarding her from all sides. Glancing back over her shoulder, she asked, "How did you do that?"

"I don't know," he said, following. "I cleaned the litter boxes and took the trash out to the garage. I couldn't get back into the house. I must have accidentally set the lock."

"You know the door from the mudroom to the garden is always unlocked, don't you?" She opened the front door.

"No, I didn't know that. You didn't tell me."

"I'm sorry."

"Apology accepted."

They paused in the foyer. Marty forced herself to look at him and then couldn't remove her gaze from his face. It was almost as if the air around them had changed. It tingled with suppressed longing...confusion. She wanted him. Her skin sizzled with this awareness. She sucked in a small breath hoping not to hyperventilate.

Jeremy flashed a sheepish smile. "I'm glad to accept your apology because you procured Wi-Fi for me a day early."

She'd helped him. *Good.* She liked that she'd helped him. "It's who you know sometimes," she said, giving her own awkward grin.

Marty hated her inexperience with men. She hated being tongue-tied, feeling clumsy and graceless. Wanting to

69

kiss him and knowing how were two different things. Golly! Why was she so naïve?

Marty bit her lip and turned away, escaping to the kitchen. "What made you decide to clean cat pans?"

He followed her there. "I thought I'd be proactive. Trying to do my bit."

"Trying to make friends?"

"That too."

She put her shoulder bag down on the counter and dropped her keys beside it. She should offer suggestions. That would be better than thinking about kisses and male body parts. "Let's see. Maybe you can brush Calliope. She loves being groomed. There's a brush in the mudroom cabinet. And Clio, the orange one, loves to sit on laps."

"And other private places."

Huh? What in the world? Did something happen in his bedroom and that's why he locked his door? "Let me talk to them again. Maybe I can get them to come around."

"You told me earlier you had no control over the cats," Jeremy reminded.

Marty scrunched her face, frowning. "Well, you're right." Suddenly she desperately wanted to help Jeremy win his inheritance. "But I can still talk to them."

"Okay. Give it a try." He hesitated a moment, surveying her face, his eyes soft and dreamy. Then he quickly turned on his heel and left the room.

Marty sat down at the table and cleared her mind. She

opened her heart and sent out greetings to Ms. Addie's six cats. She spent thirty minutes asking for them to communicate, pleading for them to talk to her.

Problem was…they all refused to respond.

Chapter Eight

Three days later Jeremy was no closer to cat friendship than he'd been on Sunday. On Monday, Jeremy found the cat brush in the mudroom cabinet after lunch. He took it upstairs where Calliope lounged on his desk, cleaning a paw, licking her long fur, and occasionally swatting at his papers and pens. He didn't know how to brush a cat so he started gently. That is until he came to a matted clump of fur and pulled too hard.

"Ryow!" Calliope clamped down on the back of his wrist with her white, pointy teeth.

"Damn!" Jeremy jerked back his arm, and the cat brush sailed through the air hitting the wall with a whack. "You stupid cat!"

"Ryow!" Calliope rounded her back and glared.

"Go on. Get off this desk!"

The calico dropped down to the floor and sauntered away with a swish of her silky tail, clearly unaffected by his attempt at friendship.

Tuesday Jinx, the sneaky black cat, tripped him, and Jeremy bumped on his butt down three steps until he came to rest on the landing. Now he had a bruise on his backside to go with the bite marks on his wrist.

Later that day, while Marty was at the grocery, Attila stormed into Jeremy's office.

"What the…?" Jeremy rose from behind the desk. Should he fear for his life?

But Attila's wrath wasn't directed at Jeremy. Poor Clio, who had been hiding under the desk, came out to meet the bully. Fur flew. The high-pitched yowling of male cats filled the office.

"My kingdom for a broom," Jeremy muttered. He lifted his eyes to the ceiling. "I'll never get any work done."

Then he stomped around the desk, clapping his hands and wishing for that broom. "Come on, break it up! Get out of here!"

The fight ended as quickly as it started, but not without a hiss or two directed Jeremy's way as the combatants departed.

Wednesday work turned ugly. One of his recruiters quit and another company put off payment for another month.

"It's getting bad, boss," Patsy told him over his cell.

"I know, I know." He rubbed his face. Frustration ate at his gut. He didn't know what to do with his business or the task of wooing a bunch of cats.

Patsy abruptly changed the subject. "That woman you're with…" She paused.

"I wouldn't say I'm *with* a woman." Good God, no! Marty's actions made it clear his kiss had not been welcome, and she'd avoided him like the proverbial plague ever since.

"You know, that woman who's taking care of the cats."

"What about her?"

"You said she could communicate with animals."

"Yes." What was Patsy driving at?

"I was wondering if she could communicate with my dog, Baby. The poor girl won't eat. I'm worried about her."

Jeremy's patience was thin. He didn't have time for games. He gritted his teeth and counted to ten. Patsy was older and single. That dog was her life. And Patsy was his lifeline at the moment. She was keeping his business together, such as it was.

"I can ask Marty," he told Patsy to humor her. "I'll let you know what she says."

They talked a few more minutes. After Patsy hung up, Jeremy couldn't face the computer screen one more minute. He shut down, closed the laptop, and escaped to the kitchen for a bottle of Coors Light.

Retreating outside, Jeremy sat down on the bench in Marty's meditation alcove. Summer sunshine warmed his back as he sat forward, resting his elbows on his knees, and dangling the cold bottle of beer between his bare legs. The sweet scent of roses assaulted his senses. He heard a bee buzz and the roar of a car on the road below the house. He sat back and took a drink.

What was he going to do? About Hamilton Staffing. About the damn cats. About the attraction he felt for the woman he *was* with—the attraction slowly pulling him in and warming his heart.

***

Gloria told Marty where to find Jeremy. That was the first communication she'd had with the cats all week. She thanked Gloria with kind thoughts, but the tortie feline slipped silently away. Marty sensed Gloria felt she'd be in trouble with the others. Why was that? What in the hell was going on?

"I see you're out here meditating," Marty said, as she approached the secluded alcove surrounded by rose bushes and shaded by a giant oak.

He looked up, his eyes gleaning. "I'm meditating in my own way."

It was Marty's turn to sit in front of him on the path with her bare legs and feet crossed. She felt his hot appraisal and blushed. She couldn't stop herself as much as she hated her reaction.

"How's it going?" she asked, hoping to cover up her self-consciousness.

He cocked his head and lowered his lashes. He didn't speak for a moment as if deciding what to say. "Things continue to be in flux."

"Meaning?" She sensed his fear.

"Work is fluid, changing daily, but still not good." He drained his bottle of beer and set the empty bottle down on the stone path. "The cats are, well, cats. Independent."

Marty looked down and rubbed a finger over the rough stones. She didn't glance up. "I'm sorry about that."

"I thought you were going to talk to the cats for me."

His statement held the tone of an accusation. Marty's

gaze shot up. "I did."

But she didn't admit the cats had rebuffed all her attempts at conversation. Geez! That was not something a purported animal communicator admitted.

"Talking to them hasn't seemed to work. These cats are more standoffish and hostile than ever."

He sounded more worried than irate. Marty couldn't blame him. From what she understood, his livelihood rested on the results of his month-long stay.

And it didn't help that she was questioning herself and her abilities. Good grief! She'd never experienced such a drought. She was silently panicked, her stomach churning with self-doubt and recrimination. She'd promised to help Jeremy, but she'd failed miserably so far.

"My admin, Patsy, asked me to ask if you could communicate with her dog. He isn't eating, and she's worried."

Marty felt this was a test from Jeremy so she'd prove herself. Maybe it was also a test of her self-confidence. "I don't usually communicate for other people."

"But you can, can't you?" His eyebrows furrowed with the question. "Or is it that you can't do it long distance?"

"I can do it. I just need a picture showing the eyes of the animal. That's all." She sounded so sure of herself, but was she? She'd never communicated with any animal other than her own pets and Ms. Addie's cats. Marty rubbed her lower lip, aware of the continuing tightness in her chest.

"If you'll try, I can get you a picture." When she

hesitated, Jeremy continued, "Think of it as a favor to me."

She couldn't turn him down. This was Jeremy. He'd kissed her, even fleetingly as a thank you for getting his Wi-Fi. Some people were like that. More touchy-feely. Not aloof and standoffish as she'd been raised. She couldn't fault him for that any more than she could forget the kiss.

"I'll try it," she said with forced enthusiasm. It would be criminal not to. Some poor animal was probably suffering.

And then it happened almost too quickly. Jeremy pulled out his iPhone from a pocket, tapped the number, spoke to Patsy, and tapped off. Seconds later, he received a text with a picture of the dog attached.

"That's Baby." He held up the iPhone for her to see the picture.

She held out her hand. "May I?"

He leaned over and handed her the iPhone. Marty held it in her hand. It was warm from his touch. She took a breath and released it, blowing it out through puffed cheeks. Then she cupped the iPhone in both hands and focused on the picture.

Baby was a Pembroke Welsh Corgi, a little girl with a comical, foxy face. Marty cleared her mind and opened her heart. She introduced herself psychically to the dog and told her why she wanted to communicate, sending her energy as pictures and feelings. Making a humming noise in her throat, Marty asked Baby if she'd talk. Then she waited.

The images came quickly. A sharp pain shot through the left side of Marty's abdomen, and she felt nauseous.

Baby said she didn't want to be sick, but her stomach hurt and her food tasted bad. The dialogue lasted only a few minutes, long enough for Marty to get a sense of what was going on. Then she thanked Baby and asked if she could talk with her again. Disconnecting with an image of waving good-bye, she lifted her head to look at Jeremy.

He gazed at her with a mixture of awe and curiosity. With her body energetically charged already, her awareness heightened, Marty experienced the lure of desire. It wasn't just on her part. Jeremy felt it too as he watched her. Damn! This was the hard part about being so psychic. She could read another's feelings—especially if she was already caught up on the same wavelength.

She was flattered. No one had ever lusted after her. She was the little girl who'd never been kissed. Remember? But his desire for her didn't mean anything. It didn't mean he loved her. It simply meant he found her attractive.

She knew herself better than most people knew themselves. She knew she could not proceed with her physical desire without love being present. Otherwise, it was simply a fleeting physical act. Love was what set the human action above the animal one. She needed to love and be loved, or she would never act upon the attraction she felt, no matter what.

"Well?"

"Well, what?" Jeremy's question drew her out of her reflection.

"Did Baby talk?"

Marty dropped her gaze. "Yes, she did."

"What did she say?"

Marty looked up and handed back the phone. "Patsy really needs to take the dog to the vet."

"I'll tell her that," he said. "No, you tell her."

Jeremy tapped the iPhone and put it up to his ear. "Yes," he said. "You talk to her." He handed back the phone. "This is Patsy."

Marty cupped the iPhone to her ear. "Hi, Patsy. Yes, Baby isn't well. You need to see a veterinarian. I can only tell you what I felt."

Marty explained about Baby's pain in her abdomen and constant nausea. How she thought her food tasted bitter and her crate smelled bad. She didn't like eating in her crate. Baby's digestive system felt empty, probably because she wouldn't eat. She needed lighter food, maybe green beans or steamed broccoli for a change. But she still liked her treats, so she wasn't completely off her food.

"You got all that?" Jeremy asked as he put away the iPhone.

"Yes. Yes, I did."

Marty tilted her head to the side. *Dang!* Baby had talked to her. Just because the cats wouldn't, didn't mean she was losing it. She smiled a secret smile.

"What?" Jeremy quizzed.

Marty found herself tearing up. She swiped off a wayward tear with the heel of her hand. Suddenly, life was better, richer. The one thing she could count on had not deserted her as she'd feared.

It was the cats. They were conspiring against both her and Jeremy. She'd been right to be suspicious. They were surely up to something. Maybe they refused to cozy up to Jeremy because of loyalty to Ms. Addie.

Uncrossing her legs, she placed the palm of her hand on the path she could push herself up and stand. Jeremy was ahead of her. He sprang to his feet and caught her free hand, pulling her up as easily as she'd just communicated with a dog hundreds of miles away.

"You're amazing," he said gazing into her eyes.

Marty held his gaze, unable to do anything else. "It's nothing," she said blowing off the compliment.

"It isn't nothing. You've helped Patsy. You're trying to help me no matter what you said earlier."

"But...."

"No, buts." He stopped her by touching her lips with a fingertip. "Come to dinner with me."

Marty felt energy shoot through the fingers of her hand still. He seemed to be as surprised by his sudden invitation as she was. She swallowed hard and stared at him.

"Tomorrow night," he continued. "When I stopped by Sydney's yesterday, Matt Branson and Chris Marks were telling me about a good restaurant at the lake."

Marty continued to stare, mesmerized by the earnest appeal in his blue eyes and the smile upon his lips. She felt like a teenager being asked to the prom.

"Let me make reservations. For the two of us. We'll be away from all this." His sentences were choppy. Breathy.

80

"We can get to know each other better."

Why did he want to get to know her? Was it to get closer to the cats? She'd already told him she'd help him. He surely didn't want to get to know her simply because he wanted to get to know her. *Duh!* He lusted after her. Wanted to take her to bed. She knew that with every ounce of psychic energy in her body.

Trouble was a woman didn't have to be psychic to understand what drove a man.

Discovering what was truly in his heart was another matter.

Chapter Nine

Marty was so kissable, standing there letting him hold her hand. Jeremy wanted her in the worst way. Did she read it in his eyes? He saw both confusion and longing in hers. He was just as confused. And the longing was blowing him out of his socks.

Slowly, Jeremy leaned toward her. He didn't want to frighten her. He simply wanted to kiss her, damn it.

She let him. She didn't pull away. Marty's lips were like honey. Encircling the back of her head with his free hand, he drew her into his kiss. Her curls were warm, grazed by the sun, and thick and heavy, hair he could lose himself in.

This time, she kissed him back. She opened her mouth to him and sighed against his lips. Long moments passed as they savored each other and the heat rose between them.

Suddenly, Jeremy felt the brush of a cat's tail on his bare legs. He groaned. Something dropped onto the top of his Nikes and rolled off. He opened one eye, tilted their heads, still kissing her, so he could peek at his feet. That's when he spied a gray mouse lying motionless beside them.

"Argh!" He pulled away from Marty.

"What is it?"

Her eyes were wide with shock. But now free from his embrace, she touched a fingertip to her lips as if he'd burned them with his kiss.

Jeremy swallowed his surprise and stood tall. A damn mouse wasn't going to scare the bejeebers out of him. "The cats," he managed to say a bit breathy.

Marty collected herself and looked around. "Clio." She pointed to a rose bush. "See the orange tail under there?"

The furry tail twitched, as if laughing at them.

Jeremy grasped both of Marty's hands and pulled her around the offending mouse. She stepped over it, and Jeremy urged her to sit beside him on the garden bench.

"You didn't answer me." He squeezed her fingers.

"We were interrupted."

Her cheeks flamed almost the same color as her hair. They were sitting so near he smelled the clean scent of lavender on her skin. Jeremy fought the impulse to kiss her again. But not before he got her answer.

"We were *rudely* interrupted." He eyed the mouse. "Come to dinner with me."

At that moment, the miniature lion appeared on the path and drew their attention. He swaggered toward them as if he were the king of the world.

"He's on a mission," Marty said in a whisper.

The little mouse was not dead. It moved, righted itself, and started to scamper away. That's when Attila caught it. He didn't pat it with a paw, let it go and catch it again as cats did when playing. He simply devoured the pour creature right there. In the middle of the path. In front of them. Jeremy heard the crunch of little mouse bones. In a minute, the animal was gone. Not even a tail or a piece of fur remained.

Attila shot them an evil eye, turned on his four paws, and strutted away as arrogantly as he'd come.

***

Luckily, Jeremy's appetite wasn't ruined by Attila's display of cat appetite, and he'd made reservations for the next night at The Deck, the swanky restaurant at Lake Lodge. As advertised, it was Legend's one and only fine dining experience.

Marty had never been there and was excited to go. She wore her Sunday skirt and blouse. It wasn't as if she had a lot to choose from. Her closet was slim because she had no need for fancy clothes. Jeremy wore his expensive business suit and was so handsome Marty's heart ached just looking at him.

He'd kissed her…twice. He'd invited her to dinner. Out on an actual date. A heady sense of newness and excitement enveloped her and knotted her stomach as they drove to the lake in Jeremy's high-powered sports car.

What would her life be like with Jeremy in it for real? Not because of Ms. Addie's money and the cats, but because of her. Because he wanted to be with her. Her head swirled with all the impossible dreams she'd never allowed herself to dream.

Lake Lodge was outside Legend overlooking the lake. It was built of logs, like a giant log cabin, with all the heavenly smells of the woods and the mountains crafted into its core. The property was historic and old, recently brought to life by Brad Matthews and his wife Suzie.

Jeremy and Marty entered the spacious lobby with its massive hotel desk and climbed the roughhewn log staircase leading to a second story landing. To their right was the dining room. A hostess, who seated them on the outside porch with the lake in the foreground and mountains providing an imposing backdrop, greeted them.

The Deck took its name from the wraparound porch. It was a lovely place to dine with its rustic chairs and wooden tables covered by white tablecloths and set with fine china and crystal. A gentle breeze reminded Marty she was outside, but the shade of the overhanging roof made the outdoor seating fresh and cool.

"Would you like a bottle of wine?" Jeremy scanned the drink list.

Marty was by no means a connoisseur. Heck, she'd only recently started drinking wine on a regular basis. Even then, taking that first drink had been hard, given her strict Methodist upbringing. Ms. Addie had said, though, God gave man wine so he could experience heaven in a glass. "I like Pinot Noir, but you pick."

The waitress brought a bottle of wine and let Jeremy taste it. He savored it, rolling it around in his mouth, and then nodded, ordering it. Marty let him select the dinner salad—mixed baby greens and grape tomatoes drizzled with onion vinaigrette—and the entrée—grilled salmon smothered with caramelized mandarin orange sauce served over cream cheese grits. All of which sounded delicious, terribly fattening, and extremely expensive.

After the waitress departed with their order, Marty sat back to survey Jeremy's face as he sipped his wine. How could it be that in such a short time she'd grown used to having him in the house? Hearing him in the office. Cleaning up the kitchen with him after a meal. She didn't like the familiarity that was growing within her. Not when he wasn't making any progress with the cats and would be gone in three weeks.

"You've got cat hair all over your coat," she remarked, just noticing it. Why hadn't he used the lint brush she'd given him?

He glanced at his lapel. "Damn cats."

Marty smiled at him, reached over, and picked a few hairs from his sleeve. It was an intimate gesture that caught them both off guard. Her heart did more than its usual flutter, starting to pound like gangbusters within her chest.

"I'm sorry." She dropped her hand and glanced away. Why did she make a habit of looking away? Why couldn't she meet his eyes?

"It's not your fault," Jeremy told her. "I draped the coat over the back of my desk chair before leaving. This morning I shooed Tinkerbelle off the chair. It must be her hair."

"Good old Tinkerbelle." Marty smiled to herself.

"I think she's your favorite."

She pressed her lips together and gazed at the ceiling, considering his question. "I'm not sure. I've never really thought about it because they all are individuals with their own quirks."

"They're pains in the ass, if you ask me."

"I'm sorry it's not going well for you." She felt the need to verbalize his disappointment.

Leaning back, Jeremy turned a flat gaze on her. "They must read my distrust of them and my disgust at this whole, stupid process."

Marty recognized the sinking of her stomach and the sudden oppressive feeling of guilt. If it wasn't for her talent and Ms. Addie's wish to stick her nose into people's business, trying to stir up change and control events even after her death, Jeremy wouldn't be in this position.

"I've tried to talk to them." Marty was candid. "But they have stopped communicating with me. I don't think they want to hear anything I have to say."

"Seriously?"

"Yes. That's why I was glad to find out I could communicate with Patsy's dog. I was afraid I'd lost my ability."

"Patsy's dog is doing much better today."

"Oh, I'm glad!" Marty brightened a little.

"She took the dog to the vet this morning. The vet did an x-ray and blood work. Turns out Baby had not passed a stool."

"That's probably the source of the pain I experienced in her stomach." It was nice to have her readings verified.

"The vet gave Baby an injection for upset stomach and prescribed a bland diet. Patsy wanted me to thank you for your advice, or she might not have gone."

"Well, that's the first thing a pet owner should do, but I'm glad it turned out well for Patsy and Baby."

Jeremy leaned forward and skimmed a fingertip along Marty's jaw line. "You're good at this communicating." His eyes were bright and glossy. This time Marty couldn't look away, mesmerized by the intensity of his gaze. "Why don't you do it for other people? I bet you could make money offering your services."

"Ms. Addie always wanted me to try." Her nerve endings tingled where his finger lingered along her jaw. Her mouth was dry, her throat growing thick. "But, well, I just am not sure of myself."

"I don't see why not."

"My self-confidence has never been very strong." She was breathless. He was kissable close. Would he kiss her here? In public? "My parents, especially my father, criticized me all my life, calling me 'weirdo.'"

"You didn't deserve that."

"No. No, I didn't. Ms. Addie showed me that."

Jeremy dropped his hand and sat back. Marty could breathe again.

"My life was different. I was a cocky son-of-a-gun for most of it, even after my mother deserted us. My dad thought I could do no wrong."

Jeremy shifted in his chair as if he couldn't get comfortable. He suddenly looked distracted. When he finally met her gaze, he said, "Recently I've begun to doubt myself."

"Not about the cats, surely?"

"About the cats and so much more. What if I run my father's business into the ground? He trusted me. I can't let him down."

"You're not letting him down."

Leaning in, Jeremy placed a hand across her wrist. "You've got to do something for me, Marty," he said lowering his voice. "You've got to tell Graham Winchester the cats don't hate me. If you don't, by the time I get my inheritance, I could be fifty-years-old, and it will be too late to save my father's company."

The fingers that seconds earlier had caressed her cheek suddenly felt as hard and confining as the meanest handcuffs.

She'd tried talking to the cats. That she could do for Jeremy. But, God help her, she couldn't lie for him.

Chapter Ten

The night hadn't gone well. After Jeremy had pleaded for Marty's help, she'd clammed up. The light had snuffed from her eyes. She'd sat back in the chair and wouldn't meet his gaze. She wouldn't answer him either.

Did she think he'd kissed her and asked her to dinner simply to sweet-talk her into helping him?

He hadn't been trying to influence her when he'd kissed her. He *had* wanted to kiss her. In fact, he had a growing suspicion she could become more to him than a goofy animal communicator. He'd seen her tenderness and caring. To him. To the cats. To his administrative assistant back in Louisville. Marty had been able to allay Patsy's fear for her dog. Giving someone peace of mind was no mean accomplishment.

Jeremy needed some of that peace. He needed to blow away the pressures of his job and the necessity to carry on as his dad would expect. Weariness seeped into his bones. His head ached. And maybe his soul.

At home they stood together in the entrance foyer at the foot of the stairs. "Good night," Marty said.

He gazed into her liquid eyes, wishing things had not gone so terribly awry. "Good night."

"I enjoyed dinner." Her voice was soft.

"We'll go again."

"Sure. Sounds good."

They held each other's attention for a heartbeat, and then when he didn't say anything, Marty turned and fled up the staircase. He watched her go, unsure of how to call her back. Life was crappy right now. He needed a drink, something stronger than a glass of wine. He needed a million dollars. And damn if he didn't need Marty in his bed tonight to anesthetize his pain.

Jeremy followed Marty slowly up the steps. As he was going up, Jinx scurried down. Tinkerbelle sat at the top of the stairs staring at him. She made a little "jrrrring" sound of welcome.

"Hey," he muttered at the cat.

The door to Marty's third floor suite shut loudly. Sighing as he reached the top landing and rounded the corner, Jeremy stood a moment. Tinkerbelle twirled around his legs, and for once he was too distracted to shoo her away.

Instead of heading to the sterile, cold white master bedroom, Jeremy detoured to the library to drown his sorrows in work. He flicked on the overhead light and crossed the floor to the cherry desk. The desktop was empty.

His paperwork was there where he'd neatly stacked it this afternoon. His leather binder with his calendar entries rested beside the papers. But the space where his Mac had sat was bare. The power cord had been unplugged and was missing too.

Fear, as sharp and ragged as a knife, stabbed him in the

gut. He raked his fingers through his hair.

He'd been robbed.

What was he going to do now?

***

Matt Branson, Legend police officer, stood at the office door, notepad in hand. "Are you sure your laptop was on your desk?"

"Yes!" How many times did Jeremy have to tell this guy the same thing?

Marty stood by the window her eyes as big as saucers, worry written all over her face. She bit her lower lip and knotted her hands in front of her. She hadn't said a word.

"Marty, did you see it on the desk tonight?" Branson asked.

She averted her gaze. "Ah, no. Not tonight. But Jeremy always keeps it there. I've never seen him use it anywhere else, unless he packs it up and takes it to Sydney's."

"Could you have left it at Sydney's?"

"No!" What part of stolen couldn't this guy figure out?

"Have you looked in your bedroom? In the rest of the house?"

"No!" Jeremy gritted his teeth. "The laptop was on the top of the desk when we left the house for dinner."

Branson wrote on his notepad. "Did you find any evidence that the house had been broken into?"

Wasn't that the job of the police?

Small towns! Jeremy hated them more than ever at the moment.

"The doors were locked when we came home," Marty said softly. "But anyone who knew Ms. Addie knew she kept the door to the garden unlocked at all times."

"Do you still keep it unlocked?"

"Yes," Marty replied. "I've tried to keep her house as she did. Sentimental, I guess."

Branson sighed. "So anyone could have opened that door and gained entrance to the house."

"Yes," Marty said with a nod. She glanced at Jeremy. "I'm so sorry."

Sorry didn't help him. Jeremy seethed with anger, his stomach twisting with pain. Could his life get any worse? Cats. A crazy great-aunt and a crazier cat woman who'd gotten under his skin. A business that was going under. Now this. His Mac was gone and so was the beginning of a proposal he'd worked on all day to get himself out of this mess without the need of Ms. Addie's money.

"What kind of laptop is it?"

"Only a fifteen-inch MacBook Pro with retina display worth two thousand dollars brand new."

"I guess you had the data backed up."

Jeremy's heart tumbled. "No." His voice trailed off as the sharp accusation of the policeman's gaze hit him in the face. "I didn't back it up to the cloud today. I was in a hurry. Anyone who got the laptop will have access to my client list, the names of my contractors, and my financials.

Everything."

The frightening feeling of doom circulated in his head and in his stomach. Jeremy sank into the chair behind the desk, his hands gripping the arms of the swivel chair.

"I see," Branson said, noting something else in his pad. "Marty, let me take a look out back, will you?"

"Sure."

Before they could get away, Jeremy asked, "Are you going to fingerprint the desk?" It was an obvious step to him, but what did he know about crime fighting? He was a recruiter, for God's sakes.

"I doubt it will do much good because so many people had access to the house. Our best bet is to notify our 'sources' to keep their eyes open. And if you two can think of anything else relevant, I'll be glad to come back."

A dead end. His whole life had disintegrated in the space of a dinner date, and this clown was not going to do anything.

"Let me show you out," Marty offered. She flashed Jeremy a look of sympathy as she turned to leave.

Jeremy cut loose with a string of swear words into the now empty room. Leaning forward, elbows on the top of the desk, Jeremy covered his face with his hands. What in the hell was he going to do?

Minutes passed as he tried to gain control of his emotions and ease the tightness in his chest. Suddenly he heard a thump and a "jrrring" sound. He sensed a cat was nearby. Opening his eyes, he stared into the furry face of

Gloria, the old cat with the orange stripe down the bridge of her nose.

"What do you want?"

The cat merely stared. He stared back. She took a step forward and ducked her ear against his arm, rubbing it.

"Go away. You'll make my eyes itch."

Gloria didn't leave. She sat there next to him purring, her motor running full force. He didn't need an overly friendly cat. Not now.

Yet, something prompted him to reach for the animal. He sat back and drew the cat into his arms. She purred even louder, if that was possible. Her front paws rested on his shirt, and she began kneading him—claws in, claws out—like a kitten with a mother cat.

Strangely, the warmth of the tortie cat, soothing purr, and the motion of its claws comforted him. This was peace. An odd peace. Shutting his eyes again, Jeremy simply lived in the moment.

He'd been like this sometime in his past. Hurting. His mother and father arguing in another room, but loud enough for him to hear. He remembered it now. In this house. The visit with his great-aunt. The boredom of a pre-teen boy wishing to be home playing basketball with friends. The big fight between his parents. The frosty drive back to Kentucky. His mother leaving.

And he remembered this cat. Only she had been a kitten then. A very friendly kitten that had slept in his bed and played with him, batting a string and chasing a ball, helping him ease the tedium of his family's visit. And comforting him when he needed a friend.

"You're that same cat, aren't you?"

The purr grew louder as if in affirmation.

Chapter Eleven

Marty couldn't go inside after Matt left. She was too torn up. Too worried the theft of Jeremy's laptop would ruin his business. And she could do nothing about it. She was powerless as she'd always been. She couldn't make her dad love or understand her. Now she couldn't help Jeremy in his time of need.

And she wanted to help him so badly. She wanted to see the light shine in his eyes and the smile spread across his face. She didn't want his eye to tick from tension. Or his lips to draw into a thin line from anxiety.

If she had money, she'd give it to him. If she could convince the cats to give him a chance, she'd do that. By herself, she could not do a thing to help him.

Sitting in her favorite spot on the bench surrounded by the scent of roses, Marty shut her eyes to the already dark night. She wiped a tear from her eye and breathed deeply, stilling her body and soul.

"I allow every physical, mental, emotional and spiritual problem, and inappropriate behavior based on old feelings of failure to disappear quickly," she said in a hushed voice, "and I ask for God's Love and Light to fill that space."

She said this prayer often, requesting the strength she could not find within herself. Ms. Addie always said God worked in mysterious ways. A person had to seek help. "Ask, and it shall be given you."

Marty wasn't sure it worked. But she often prayed, especially when she felt no hope.

And then five of the six cats were sitting on the path in front of her. Marty sensed their arrival. One by one. She opened her eyes after they were there to see their furry shapes in the shadows. Sending an image of welcome, she waited.

And then they started talking all at once.

"Jinx saw him," Clio said, "and followed him."

"He shouldn't have come into the house," Calliope purred. "He scared me."

Tinkerbelle rubbed against Marty's legs. "He shouldn't have done it. He was bad."

Marty felt their agitation. Could they have seen the burglar?

"Okay, calm down," she said to them. "Who did you see?"

Five varied cat voices replied, "Woody."

"Woody?"

Marty perceived the confirmation from all the furry felines. Even Attila joined in with a resounding "Yes."

"Wait a minute! You're telling me Woody, the gardener, came into Ms. Addie's house while we weren't here?"

"Yes!"

"Did he take Jeremy's laptop?"

That's why they were so excited and talkative. The cats had witnessed the crime. They'd seen who stole Jeremy's laptop. She'd stumbled upon the solution to the mystery thanks to the cats. But why did they tell her?

They read her thoughts.

"We know you like him," Tinkerbelle artlessly said as if that was enough.

But more troubled Marty. "Why did you quit talking to me?"

"Darling," Calliope purred, "We don't want you to leave us."

Of course! It was so simple. If Jeremy received his inheritance, the cats thought they would lose Marty and their home. That's why they'd stopped communicating.

She believed the cats. Heck, she'd heard them in her own heart and head. Yet, others would not think her word was good enough. "How am I going to prove Woody took the laptop?"

Attila strutted down the pathway. "I hit him," he said proudly.

"Hit him?"

"Attila tried to stop the bad guy," Calliope purred again. "Attila was so brave."

"Woody got away, but not before Attila struck him with a paw," Tinkerbelle chimed in.

"And scratched him hard," Clio said.

"Oh, Attila, you're wonderful!" Marty scooped Attila

off the path and into her arms. She buried her face into his fur, showering him with kisses. "Thanks to you, we can get Jeremy's laptop back."

The self-important Maine coon had his dignity. He didn't like Marty cuddling him and squirmed in her arms trying to escape.

"Okay, I'll put you down," Marty said to Attila. "But we must all go together to tell Jeremy!"

***

What the...? Jeremy looked up to see Marty standing at the office door holding Tinkerbelle. Around her legs congregated the other cats, all but Gloria because she was still in his arms.

"Jeremy." Marty's voice held a hopeful note, her eyes gleaming. "May we come in?"

She was adorable there in the doorway surrounded by those pesky felines. He offered a weak smile in reply to her question. Marty let Tink drop to the floor. The cats scampered into the room and scattered under his desk or jumped onto the five-story cat condo by the window. He felt encircled by them.

"I know who took your laptop." Marty followed the cats into the room.

Jeremy released Gloria and stood up. Hope glimmered in his heart. "You do?"

"It was Woody, the gardener."

"Woody?" Jeremy's let out a breath. "How do you know?"

"The cats told me."

She was so matter-of-fact, so sure of herself. "Oh, I see." He sunk down into the chair. Who would believe her? She was the crazy cat woman, after all.

Marty's eyes suddenly dulled with doubt. Was she wondering if he'd believe her too? At that moment, it was important for him *to* believe in Marty, in her abilities. In her. Somehow he realized he faced a crossroads. Would he have faith, for once in something outside himself? In something he couldn't control? Or would he continue on the path he was traveling—alone with no one to rely on but himself? At the moment, it was a path he wasn't traveling very well.

Suddenly nothing else mattered except trusting her. "I believe you," he said with a smile.

She drew a shuddering breath. "You do?"

"Yes." He stood again and came around the desk. He caught her arms and pulled her to him, searching her eyes for assurance. "I believe you, but how will we convince the police?"

"Quite simply really." Her face held an amused look. "Attila tried to stop him. He attacked Woody, who should have very distinctive cat scratches somewhere on his body."

Unbelievable.

Jeremy glanced down at his feet where the monster cat squatted on his haunches. "I owe you one, Attila my man."

Marty giggled. She had such a lyrical laugh that cut right

into his heart.

"I owe you too, Marty. I owe you big time."

"Oh, it's nothing."

"It's everything to me."

He drew her to him and kissed her deeply. It was more than his other simple pecks of gratitude. For him, this one held more meaning. Something akin to love.

After a moment's hesitation, Marty curled her arms around his neck, sighing, and melted into him. Into his heart. His soul. This woman was nothing like his mother or Lauren. Her whole life spoke of sincerity and love. Of tenderness and compassion. Jeremy would do well to have all that in his life.

They lingered for a long moment kissing until they came up for breath, but he wouldn't let Marty slip from his arms. He held her there near him, and brushed a red curl from her forehead. He felt her heart beating heavily against her chest. He wanted her, but he wouldn't have her tonight. This was Marty, after all, as skittish as her cats. He wanted her to know him better. Trust him.

He wanted to see where his path would lead if Marty joined him by his side.

"First things first," he said gazing into her eyes. "The laptop. But once that's settled, I want you and me to get to know each other better."

"You do?" She gasped as if she didn't understand his meaning.

"As boyfriend and girlfriend." It seemed such an

archaic concept in this day and age. "Only if *you* want to know me better. But it has nothing to do with those damn cats."

"I'd like that," she whispered, snuggling closer. "You know something? The cats wouldn't have told me about Woody if they didn't like you."

"What?"

She looked up and gave him a mischievous smile. "So, I'll just have to tell Graham to give you the money, but maybe not for three more weeks so I can keep you around."

"That's wicked. Nonetheless, I think I'm beginning to love you, Marty Fields."

"I love you too, Jeremy."

The way she said his name turned him on so fast that it was all he could do to stop himself from sweeping her off her feet and carrying her to bed. But he didn't. His hug tightened, and she tucked her head under his chin.

How could things have changed for him so drastically in less than a week?

It was weird. Impossible. As weird and impossible as having his own real-life Dr. Doolittle.

Jan Scarbrough

Epilogue

Matt Branson didn't believe them at first, but after Marty told him what to look for, the cop agreed to call on Woody's house even though it was after midnight.

When the doorbell rang after two hours of stressful waiting, Marty rushed to answer it. She brought Branson back with her, and he was carrying Jeremy's MacBook.

"You got it!" Jeremy sprang to his feet and met the policeman at the door to accept the laptop. "Thank you, man."

"It was in the trunk of his car," Branson informed them. "And just like you said, Marty, the kid had a big scratch mark on his leg. He tried to tell me he'd been attacked by an alley cat, but when I pointed out the six claw marks that only Attila could make, he came clean immediately."

"I owe you one," Jeremy said.

"Just doing my job," Branson replied. "Thank Marty here. She's the one who figured it out."

"It's Attila you all should be thanking," Marty said. "He protected the house when we were gone."

"May I suggest you start locking that back door? I wouldn't be doing my job well," Branson said, "if I didn't tell you that you're inviting trouble with it unlocked."

"Point taken," Marty agreed and glanced at Jeremy. "I

guess things will have to change with Ms. Addie gone."

"Yes," Jeremy concurred. "Things around this house are going to change. Big time. Just you wait and see, Marty. Just you wait and see."

Legend Post-Dispatch
Two months later in the business section

Ms. Marty Fields announces the opening of her shop in The Angel's Smoky Mountain Metaphysical Center, located at Pigeon Forge, Tennessee, where she will take half-hour appointments as an animal communicator.

***

Legend Post-Dispatch
Six months later in the society section

Martha Fields, a professional animal communicator, is to be married to Jeremy Hamilton, owner of Hamilton Staffing located in Louisville, Kentucky. Ms. Fields is the daughter of Mr. and Mrs. Nate Fields of Legend, Tennessee. Mr. Hamilton is the son of the late David Hamilton of Louisville, Kentucky. A June wedding is planned.

THE END

AUTHOR'S NOTE

An animal communicator, sometimes also called a pet psychic, is a person who has the gift and/or the skill to communicate telepathically with all other species. Several years ago, I took a "how to" workshop from a local animal communicator. I was terrible at speaking with pets, but fascinated. Never fear! A writer can do anything she wants simply by becoming that character she creates in a book. So when I chose my heroine for Heart to Heart, I gave her the ability to talk and listen to animals.

And if you think I made up the part about Ms. Addie's cats, I didn't. I found it right there on the Internet—a news article about cats receiving $250,000 and a house in a will. Facts, they say, are stranger than fiction.

For this novella, I consulted two books: *The Language of Animals* by Carol Gurney and *The Language of Miracles* by Amelia Kinkade. I also received a reading from a local animal communicator, **Fredricka Chambers**, about my dog. She provided accurate, helpful information, which I acted on and the issues were resolved.

I also suspended my disbelief—which is an essential ingredient for any kind of storytelling.

ABOUT JAN SCARBROUGH

Jan Scarbrough is the author of the popular Bluegrass Reunion series, writing heartwarming contemporary romances about home and family, single moms and children, and if the plot allows, about another passion—horses. Living in the horse country of Kentucky makes it easy for Jan to add small town, Southern charm to her books and the excitement of a horse race or a big-time, competitive horse show.

Jan also contributes to the bestselling Ladies of Legend series in collaboration with writers Maddie James, Janet Eaves and Magdalena Scott. Set in fictitious Legend, Tennessee, these romances bring together the small town family atmosphere so many readers enjoy.

Leaving her contemporary voice behind, Jan wrote *My Lord Raven,* a medieval story of honor and betrayal and *Freely Given,* a collection of short stories about women attempting to preserve their autonomy in the Middle Ages. Her paranormal Gothic romance, *Tangled Memories,* was a Romance Writers of America (RWA) Golden Heart finalist. *Timeless* is her latest paranormal romance.

A member of Novelist, Inc., Jan has published with Kensington, Five Star, ImaJinn Books, Resplendence Publishing, and Turquoise Morning Press.

Other Books by Jan Scarbrough

Visit Jan at www.janscarbrough.com

You can also follow Jan on Twitter at https://twitter.com/romancerider.

If you enjoyed Jan Scarbrough's *Heart to Heart* please consider telling others and writing a review on sites such as **Amazon** and **Goodreads**.

Other books in The Winchesters of Legend, TN series
Santa's Kiss
A Groovy Christmas
The Reunion Game

You might also enjoy these other books by Jan Scarbrough

Betting on Love
Kentucky Cowboy
Kentucky Woman
Kentucky Flame
Kentucky Bride
Kentucky Heat
Kentucky Groom
Kentucky Rain
Kentucky Blue Bloods

Read the excerpt!

THE REUNION GAME

Chapter One

There was no way sex with Graham Winchester was as good as she remembered.

Jane Smith stood alone in the crowded Legend VFW hall where her fifteenth-year high school reunion was in full swing around her. She held a plastic wineglass of California merlot, which gave her something to do with her hands, smiled at Betty Jo, the clerk from the Piggly Wiggly who waved from across the dance floor, and thanked her lucky stars for the relative darkness on the periphery of the dance floor.

He'd arrived. Heat surged through Jane's body. Graham Winchester—senior class president, debate team captain, yearbook staff member, valedictorian and Mr. Most Likely to Succeed—had finally come home to Legend.

For fifteen years, she fantasized about Graham. For fifteen years, she remembered that one night alone with him in the back seat of his family Chevy. Sure, it had been cliché. Graduation night. One thing leading to another. Each going their separate ways the next day.

She'd put him behind her and gotten on with her life. College first and then back to Legend to teach high school English. When her mom was diagnosed with cancer, she cared for her. After years as a volunteer at the county dog pound, she founded Legend's non-kill Pet Rescue. Last year, she'd quit teaching and opened a bookstore.

Yet she'd never forgotten Graham.

Cold, hard truth washed over Jane as she watched from the shadows. For all she accomplished, she was still stuck in high school. Her love life sucked. It'd been on hold for much too long.

She must exorcise the demon Graham had become and put him out of her mind and heart for the last time.

***

You can never go home again.

The cliché rang in Graham's ears along with the sounds of Michael Jackson's *Thriller* pulsating from a DVD player set up on a folding table. What in the blazes was he doing here? He didn't belong in Legend any more.

The dimly lit VFW Hall was very different from the trendy, super chic Times Square dance clubs he usually frequented. Decked out with feathery table decorations, sprinkles of glitter and mirror balls throwing colored lights on the dance floor, the rented hall looked outdated and shabby like his memories of middle school sock hops.

"Graham Winchester?"

He hardly recognized Legend High's former All-State defensive back. Clint Roberts had put on a few pounds. When Dawn Smith dumped him to go out with Clint, he shouldn't have been surprised. After all, football was a big thing in Tennessee.

Bracing for a rush of old resentment, Graham extended his hand. "Clint, how are you?"

"Fine." Always a big guy, Clint towered over him. He transferred the bottle of beer he carried to his left hand and grasped Graham's. "Man, you don't look a day older. Can you believe it's been this long? That big city life must agree with you."

The bitterness Graham expected to feel failed to materialize. "Thanks, but I *feel* older."

"Know what you mean." Clint nodded. "So how's it goin'?"

"Can't complain."

"Yeah, same here. Hey, I heard you wrote a book. Claudia was telling me."

"Claudia?"

"Yeah, you remember, Claudia Ridgeway, now Claudia Jones."

Oh, his senior class secretary. A real one-person pep squad. How quickly he'd forgotten.

"You're the biggest thing that's happened to Legend since the Dragons won the National Finals last fall," Clint said. "You and Dawn comin' home, the two of you voted most likely to succeed. It's the talk of the town."

Most likely to succeed? What a joke. His law career was at a standstill. Sure, he'd written one novel, but as his agent pointed out more than once, he was deep in the throes of writer's block with the deadline looming.

Graham shifted his stance. He was a fake, but he'd be damned if he'd let his classmates in on the horrible truth.

111

"What are you doing now?" Graham asked politely.

"Sellin' cars."

"Cars?"

"Yep, own the Ford dealership in town."

"That's impressive."

"Make a damn good living too. Certainly can't complain."

"I see." Graham shifted again and glanced around the darkened hall. "Are you married?"

"Hell, no. What about you?"

"No.

"Smart man," Clint shot back.

Graham didn't know how smart he was, but he nodded in response.

"So why haven't you gotten married?"

Clint's question caught Graham off guard. He took a deep breath, considering his answer. "Guess I never found the right woman," he said.

Clint nodded. "I found the right woman, but she up and left town fifteen years ago."

"For another man?"

"Nope. Hollywood."

"You mean you wanted to marry Dawn Smith?"

"We talked about it," Clint admitted, "but one day she took off to California and I went on to play ball for

Tennessee."

"You must be bitter." The thought came out of his mouth before he realized it.

Clint shrugged. "Hell, no. Dawn had a lot of ambition. Look at what she's done."

Graham knew all about what small-town girl, Dawn Smith, had done with her ambition. He followed her career off and on, and in the last few weeks he looked up her name on the Internet. Dawn's official web site said she worked in a soap opera for five years and then graduated to sitcoms. She was nominated for an Emmy, and had recently starred in her first motion picture. The girl from Legend, Tennessee, had become a movie star.

"You're a good man," Graham said, looking at Clint in a new way. "Did Dawn come tonight?"

"Sure thing. Haven't you noticed the crowd over by the bar?"

The group near the bar parted, and Graham caught a glimpse of his one-time steady. "I can't tell much about her from here."

"She's prettier than ever," Clint said with a touch of pride. Then in a confidential tone, he offered, "Divorced too."

Graham arched an eyebrow. "Love 'em and leave 'em?"

"Yep." Clint cleared his throat and lifted the bottle to his lips.

Because the ex-football player was strangely talkative, Graham pumped him again, "Whatever happened to her twin sister Jane?"

Clint tilted his head. "You didn't keep up with her?"

"No, we never had any contact after Dawn and I…well…you know."

That was a small evasion of truth. The fact was he had a whole lot of contact with Jane on graduation night after the ceremony. In the back seat of his dad's Chevy. It was their first time together. Their first and last.

Graham's pulse revved up at the surprisingly vivid memory. After that night, schoolwork and college frat life absorbed him. He moved to New York and joined a law firm, putting Dawn, Jane and the folks in Legend behind him.

"She's here," Clint said. "See her standing over there?"

Graham sought Jane out in the dim light, remembering how she'd reluctantly shared the job of yearbook editor with him. They fought like two boxers over every caption and picture. Graham smiled at the memory. It'd been amusing to bait her. She'd taken everything so seriously. Not like her twin sister. No, Jane wasn't anything like Dawn.

Jane stood beside a man, but her posture was stiff and aloof, as if she didn't want to be with him. She wore a simple, but elegant blue dress with a high collar and short sleeves. Typical Jane. The smart twin. The one with as much natural reserve as beauty. There was something charming about the way she wore her blond hair in short, flirty curls.

"Whom is she talking to?" Graham asked.

114

"Claudia's brother, Steven. See how he's putting the moves on her? Ever since his divorce, he's trying to get her to marry him."

So Jane wasn't married either.

"Hey, watch out. Here comes Claudia!" Following his warning, the big jock turned on his heels and departed.

Graham had time for one quick breath before Claudia Ridgeway, now Jones, descended on him like an avenging angel.

***

Jane caught her breath. Claudia slowly propelled Graham around the room. They were talking to Steven, who she'd successfully shaken for the time being, but soon Claudia would bring Graham to her.

The thought of seeing Graham again made her stomach cramp. She dreaded this moment for fifteen years, anticipated it, played it over in her mind, thought it'd never take place, and longed for it.

"Jane, here you are!" Her friend pulled Graham to a halt right in front of her. "Graham's asked about you."

"Hello, Jane."

Graham's deep voice engulfed her. Jane clasped his outstretched hand with her icy fingers, finding his grasp warm and strong, and much more masculine than she remembered. He smiled, and pleasure jolted through her.

Suddenly tongue-tied, like a worshiping adolescent, Jane stared into his dusky eyes, completely blown away by his stature and confident presence. He was dazzling. His

115

brown hair was a bit too long and his eyelashes, sinful. She'd forgotten how long and luscious they were. Too long to waste on a man.

He was nothing like she remembered. He was much better. The feelings she'd thought dead resurrected in that moment.

"Hey, Graham. Long time no see." Her words sounded childish.

"It *has* been a long time. You look wonderful."

His gaze ran up and down her body as if her dress were made of plastic wrap. Her face grew hot, and she blessed the dimness surrounding the dance floor.

"You don't look bad yourself," she said as he released her hand.

It was hard to see what he wore, but she could tell by the cut of the expensive cloth it was a designer suit. His power tie was knotted just right and his crisp white shirt, perfect. He smelled good too, wearing a manly scent of sandalwood and leather.

"Claudia tells me you own a bookstore now," Graham said.

"Yes." His voice was pure silk while hers sounded like backwoods East Tennessee. "I carry your bestseller."

He avoided her eyes. "I'm still not accustomed to hearing people say that."

"It's a terrific novel. You're a talented writer. A book on the New York Times list is quite an accomplishment."

"Thanks."

Are you married? Do you have a lover? Have you missed Legend? Or me? Jane wanted to ask so many questions. Instead she shifted her weight to another foot and inquired as casually as possible, "So, how's life treating you?"

"Fine." His gaze wandered across her face, touching her with a pulse-pounding intimacy. "And you?"

"Oh, I've been fine." Jane captured his gaze briefly and then hastily lowered her eyes.

She was an emotional coward. Always had been where Graham was concerned. Why had she not summoned the courage to confront him about their time together? About her suspicions she'd been a poor substitute for Dawn. She should've done it sooner. Phoned him. Sent e-mail. Instead she allowed days to creep into years, always wondering, never receiving closure.

"You're not married?"

She shook her head. "No. How about you?"

"Plenty of girlfriends, but no wives."

Jane found herself holding her breath.

Graham smiled again and then lifted his gaze over her shoulder. "Here comes Claudia."

And Dawn. Jane knew it instinctively. Claudia would escort the queen to her king.

She turned slowly. Tonight her movie star sister appeared sexy in a black silk dress, stiletto pumps, adding four inches to her height, and an updo that had taken poor Mary Maloney at Mane Locks three hours to create. But Jane refused to be awestruck by Dawn. Her identical twin was a part of her life, a sometimes irritating, sometimes lovable part.

Older by four minutes, Dawn was the first-born and all their lives her sister had taken the lead. Jane willingly let her. With the same wavy blond hair, blue eyes and dimpled smiles, they'd been adorable Shirley Temple-like children, properly spoiled by their doting parents.

Yet for all their physical similarities, they were different. Dawn was given all the out-going genes, the popularity ones, genes that counted for something in a small town. Whereas, she was naturally shy, and endowed with a stubborn streak that made her want to prove just how different she was from Dawn.

Maybe that's why she became the brainy twin. The responsible one. The one who stayed in town after their dad died of a heart attack and nursed their mother through her long illness.

"Graham, darling!"

Graham turned. "Hello, Dawn."

Dawn embraced Graham. The drama played out before the watching classmates—the beautiful Hollywood actress and the bestselling author.

Jane retreated to a table and sank into a chair. She gulped big breaths as if she'd run a marathon. Dawn looked happy to see Graham again. And her sister was now free. No, she couldn't have designs on Graham, could she?

118

The Time of My Life from the movie *Dirty Dancing* came over the loud speakers. She loved that movie when she was a preteen, identifying with the character of Baby, the shy heroine who had the courage to go after the hunky dance instructor. Why couldn't she be like Baby?

Graham ushered Dawn to the dance floor and swung her sister into the swaying mambo steps they learned at ballroom dancing lessons in the eighth grade—steps right from the script of her favorite movie.

Jane curled her fingers into a fist. No, she wasn't a mealy-mouthed teenager any longer. She was an adult and tired of dreaming about Graham Winchester and what might have been.

Jane put her palms flat down on the table. Slowly she pushed herself to her feet. Surprising even herself, Jane marched across the dance floor.

Like Patrick Swayze in the movie, Graham twirled Dawn around and lowered her, bending her back and leaning over her in an imitation kiss. They lingered like that, staring into each other's eyes, their lips inches apart.

"Excuse me." Jane tapped Graham's shoulder. "I believe this is my dance."

Thank you!

For purchasing this book from

Saddle Horse Press

Jan Scarbrough

Invitation for a free ebook

You have recently purchased a paperback copy of Heart to Heart. Maybe you bought it as a birthday or Christmas gift and might like to read it yourself.

If you send me via email a copy of your receipt, I will send you one of the following free ebook versions:

iBook

Kindle

PDF

How do you do this?

Simply scan the receipt from your print purchase or even easier, make a screenshot from your Amazon or B&N receipt. Via email, send the copy of your receipt to me at jan@janscarbrough.com.

.

59637563R00081

Made in the USA
Charleston, SC
08 August 2016